Tall Tales & Scuttlebutt

A Doce Blant Pirate Anthology

PIRATE ANTHOLOGY
by various DOCE BLANT AUTHORS

Copyright ©2020 by Doce Blant Publishing

All rights reserved.

This book or part thereof may not be reproduced in any form by any means, electronic or mechanical, including photocopy, recording, or otherwise, or by any information storage and retrieval system, except as may be expressly permitted in writing from the publisher as provided by the United States of America copyright law. Requests for permission should be addressed to Doce Blant Publishing, Attn: Rights and Permissions Dept., 1600-B Dash Point Road, #1040, Federal Way, WA 98023

Published by
Doce Blant Publishing, Federal Way, WA, 98023
www.doceblantpublishing.com

Cover by Fiona Jayde Media
Interior Design by The Deliberate Page

ISBN: 978-1-7353508-5-1

Printed in the United States of America

www.doceblant.com

This is a fictional work. Names, characters, places and incidents are the product of the author's imagination and used fictitiously. Any resemblance to actual persons, living or dead, including events and locations, is entirely coincidental.

Contents

A Pirate's Life for me (P. J. Roscoe)... 1

Tulum (Teresa Carol) 11

Back from the Dead Red (Marti Melville) 21

Lost Among Waves (P. J. Roscoe) 33

And Other Ships Flee (Marti Melville)................ 41

The Stupidest Mistake Ever Made by Pirates (David K. Bryant)...45

Avast (Ren Cummins)..............................53

Treasure (T. L. Vale)................................81

The Entity (A. M. Crane) 89

A Hatchling's Time to Fly (Ren Cummins) 99

Mickey Mathews and Barnacle Jimmy (Jim Sargent) 123

Laguna Rana Mugidora (Barnacle Bill Bedlam) 135

The Lure (Kiri Callaghan) 141

About the Authors................................. 161

About Doce Blant.................................165

A Pirate's Life for me...

by P. J. Roscoe

'Ahoy there, matey!'

I turn towards the shout, hand instantly going for the hilt of my sword, but the man had already passed me and was embracing a fellow pirate and his wench beside him. I stood staring at them for a moment. Their conduct was relaxed, friendly, no hint of malice or fear at being caught by his majesty's soldiers. They brazenly flaunted their piracy. I walked on, with a brief backward glance at the red-haired wench who was now giggling at some lewd remark. I may acquaint myself with her later, if I could find her again.

The street was busy. People dressed in all manner of clothing passed me, without more than a quick glance. Many were fully clad in clothes I recognized from my own brethren, and many wore the hats of status acquired to become "captain" of the ship; yet instinct told me, these men, and women, did not captain any pirate ship that I knew.

I continued following the many groups of laughing, drinking people until I finally smelt the aroma I knew so well; alcohol. I walked faster, pushing past those that stood in my way, ignoring their cries of indignation. If any dared to challenge me, it would be their undoing. None did, as I walked faster towards the one thing I knew I could count on to be true. I was wrong.

I turned a corner in the street and was faced with something I had known all of my seven and thirty years as a sailor; the stench of drink, smoke and sweating bodies. So many people wandered this street, I could barely see the road beneath their feet. Many sat or stood outside an ale house, judging from the scent of beer that invaded my nostrils; whilst others stood in crowds, talking, jesting and drinking. I headed for the inn and entered. More people crammed into the stifling area. Women and men drank together. I saw some women dressed as whores, though none seemed to be offering their wares to any pirates present, and no pirate was taking what he could. No fights. No brawls. No shouting, beyond attempting conversation. What kind of ale house is this?

I picked up the nearest glass, half drunk and smelled the contents. Ale of some sort. I drank it thirstily and went in search of another. I ordered ale from the barman who poured me a decent glass and asked for payment of which I did not understand. I showed him coin. He laughed and said, 'Yeah, okay, just this once. In the spirit of the pirate weekend, I'll let you have a pint for a silver coin!'

I knew not what he spoke of. I gave him silver for a mere drink. Is that not what occurs here in this strange place? A pirate weekend? A celebration of pirates? That seemed unlikely, as when I last recalled, pirates were hunted, condemned and hanged for our crimes, not celebrated.

I finished my drink, which I deemed satisfactory, though rum would be twice as sweet. I spied a bottle across the bar and moved to reach it. 'Hey, stay that side of the bar, mate.' A buxom wench scolded me as she marched up and pushed me back. 'I know we're busy, but we're doing the best we can. Now, what can I get you?'

I look her over admiring the figure of such a small, dainty thing. She glares back at me, waiting. She has courage this one. I like women with a bit o' fire in their belly. 'Come 'ere missy and I'll tell ye' what I want.'

She moves closer, giving me her ear. 'Rum an' your company would be pleasing to me.'

She smiles sweetly. As sweet as a plum. Good teeth. Brown eyes. A fine bosom, barely hidden beneath that bodice. 'Maybe later. For now, I'll get you that rum… Pirate.'

Pirate? She says what I am without flinching, without fear. I cannot fathom such a notion. Does the word, "pirate" not strike fear in the hearts of these people? She brings the bottle and a small glass filled with hard water. I stare at it. I have heard stories of places where water has become so cold, it hardens; I never thought to see it in a glass. It makes me feel uneasy. I tip it out before she can pour. She makes a small sound of irritation, before meeting my stare again. 'Single or double? You want coke with that?'

Single or double what? Coke? 'I'll take the whole bottle if ya' please.' I yank it out of her grasp and storm away towards the door. I hear her cry out and two men step forward, barring my way. 'Sir, I can't let you walk out with that bottle.'

Can't? Not a word I take heed of. I pull out my pistol that had remained resting in its sheath and point it at them. They do not flinch, nor appear scared of death. For a moment, I admire them, before firing. Nothing happens. No bullet propels out of the barrel. No blood oozes from a wound. Nobody dies. I glance down at my pistol searching for the reason for its lack of function. It looks the same as it had done since I took it from a dead man last year during a raid. It had never faltered in all that time, yet now, it refused me.

'Yeah, sir, put that away. Give back the bottle, pay for your drinks and leave the bar, or I call the cops.' Without preamble, he wrenched the bottle of rum from my hands, gave it back to the waiting wench who now looked at me with disgust; I was used to that look. He asked if I owed anything, and on getting a negative, he and his friend, frog-marched me out onto the street, pushing me forward, away from the door. 'Do not come back. Being a pirate is one thing. Stealing is another.'

I walked away, his words tumbling through my head. Pirate and stealing went together, yet he implied otherwise? I needed a drink. A large group of pirates and wenches stood in my way. All drank heartily and I smelled rum and whisky and ale. One wench saw me and hailed me to join them. She offered me a strange cup that crumpled when I squeezed. Glass did not do this, but she then poured a large slug of rum into it and I did not care what it was made of. I drank and drank some more.

The group spoke of going into the "festival", whatever that meant, and I followed along. They were happily offering me various drinks which were making my body sway and my mind fuddled. I'd have gone to the grave with these merry pirates, if they were indeed such. I knew not what was happening, but it would seem that "pirates" were not considered "scallywags" here. Nobody challenged me or questioned my attire. I could blend in freely and was accepted without question. A strange occurrence to be sure, but one I was not going to fathom tonight. Time was a'wastin'. I intended to enjoy myself.

I saw huge air-filled ships and a giant octopus that bounced as young children played on it. No one appeared frightened by such a monster and my new friends laughed when I spoke of it. 'It's a bouncy castle thing.' Said one. I saw no castle, but it did indeed spring back and the children appeared happy. I saw big metal arms flying around and around in a circle with more children screaming and laughing as they sat inside this strange arm-like machine. Such strangeness abounds indeed. We moved on.

We walked through some kind of a market. Small huts offered different wares to passing pirates. I saw clothes, paintings, scrolls of some sort and many smells invaded my nostrils of sweet spices. I saw weaponry which caught my eye and nobody seemed to be guarding them. I quickly headed for these to claim for myself. And then, I saw them. Beautiful women sat talking and laughing whilst offering books to pirates and wenches. Pictures caught my attention and I wandered over. I saw that one book had a picture of a pirate ship on a stormy sea and a full moon lit up the dark sky. On another I saw a pirate and his bird staring back at me which made me lean closer as he looked real to my eyes. The large book nearest to me had a woman walking towards a ghostly castle and a face watched her from the sky; it near chilled my very bones.

'Hello'.

A sweet voice caught my attention and I looked up at a woman with deep blue eyes.

'Can I help you? Do you like to read?'

Her voice was of an accent I had not heard for such a long time. As a boy I had been sent to sea by my uncle, either that or starve on the streets of Cardiff in Wales. To hear a Welsh accent, even from the north of my home country, after so long, caused me to be speechless. I point at the ghostly book nearest to me.

'Would you like me to sign it for you? What's your name, pirate?'

I nod and she does indeed write, '*Blessings, P.J. Roscoe.*' And then looks up at me expectantly.

'Erm… My name? 'Tis dangerous for a man, such as myself to give 'ye my name Missy… Pirate will do…'

She smiles warmly and does indeed write, '*pirate*' followed by an X.

'That'll be fifteen dollars please, pirate.'

Dumbstruck, I hand over money I had pick-pocketed from the group of drinkers. She smiles and hands back a note. 'That's too much. This is fine. Thank you, hope you enjoy it. Reviews are always helpful to an author…'

I smile. 'Tis good to hear your voice lass. I wish ye' well.'

I am rewarded with another smile, a nod of thanks, before she moves onto another pirate wanting her attention. I back away, drunk, unsure what to do, where to go. I look down at the book in my hand as the sun begins to set. I open it and see the pages full of words, though I know not what they say; I feel a small sense of disappointment that I cannot read as I would like to know what is written.

I move farther away from the small huts and the smell of ale invades my nostrils again. I look at the money in my hand and grin. I order ale as musicians enter a raised area and begin to sing a song of sorts. Though it is very loud and the words are not familiar to me, I realize that I am indeed, enjoying my one night a year when I am allowed to step foot on this earth. How fatuous that it be in time for a celebration of pirates on Tybee island. Yo ho ho, matey. Yo ho…

BOOKS BY P.J. ROSCOE

Echoes
Diary of Margery Blake

https://www.doceblant.com/p-j-roscoe/
http://www.pjroscoe.co.uk/

Tulum

BY TERESA L CAROL

A scream startled me awake as my traveling companion struggled to close the tall wooden gate that served as our flimsy door.

"Sophie, stop!" I rocked myself forward and lunged out of the hammock. I tripped forward to land with my face pressed against the driftwood that formed the side of the hovel that we currently claimed as home. My feet, sunk into the sand; I needed to carefully regain my footing so as not to push the makeshift wall down. The shack was composed of reclaimed boards dug into the earth and then wired into a circle wide enough to hang two hammocks. The door was a part of the wall that had been shortened so it could be peeled outward to exit and secured with a chain and padlock.

"Wait, I will come with you! Give me a chance to lock up."

Sophie turned, and stood in the moonlight, staring at me. The muscles of her body appeared carved beneath her alabaster skin; her head adorned with a braid which she had wrapped twice around her crown. "Yes, Mom!" Wind whipped her skirt and tugged at her shawl. "I'll be alright. It wasn't human; probably a panther, up in the ruins. It will stay away from the beach and the lights."

I was never sure if she was being sarcastic or playful! We were classmates at the Evergreen State College, and

I was a good 25 years older than her. "You know," I shook my head, "I'll feel better if you're not alone. We are not in the US; this is not a safe place for anyone to be isolated."

"Okay, Mom!" Pivoting, she began trudging towards the distant beach lights. The little resort, north of Tulum, hosted a number of classier shanties and a restaurant with a bar. By road, it was a little short of a mile, but it looked deceivingly closer along the shore.

The sand caused me to labor to keep my footing. The surf roared and hissed as it surged and slapped at the edge of the seashore. I wondered if a storm was coming. I looked up to see the night sky sharp with points of crystalline stars. I pushed myself closer to the water's edge where the sand was packed.

Sophie had pulled off her shawl and twirled it in the wind. There was something childlike in the way she approached life. I sighed. When had I become so cautious?

Suddenly a burly man grabbed my arm and shoved me down. He dropped on his knees over my hips. I thrashed, pushing him back as I attempted to catch my breath. I screamed, but my voice sounded like a raspy gasp.

"Donde esta?" he pulled me up and shook me.

"What?" my heart raced, and my mind struggled to understand the situation. "Where is what?"

He didn't respond to my English, rather he continued to ask me: where is it. *"Donde? Donde esta?"*

"Que?"

Glaring into my face his rancid breath caused me to draw back. His thick hands jerked me forward as he repeated, *"Donde esta?"*

Sophie tentatively stood about ten feet away, her sandals in her hand. "What is he looking for?"

"*No, se*" I looked into the glassy eyes of my attacker, emphasizing my words.

"*Mentias!*"

"I am not lying!" I stressed in an attempt to sound indignant, "I have no idea of what you are looking for."

He stood, pulling me up to my feet, then he hauled me towards the water with his bare arm around my neck. I struggled. As I attempted to pull free, he tightened his arm which slid across my mouth. I bit down.

Viciously he grabbed me and buried his face against my neck. His thick hair hung in dreads that smelled of smoke and grease. I flailed slapping and punching at him. He bit me, his teeth cut deep into my collar bone, then he jerked his head back, tearing my skin. I screamed.

Sophie rushed forward and slapped him timidly with a sandal. He released me as he lunged toward her. Shrieking, she sprinted towards the distant lights. He lumbered after her bellowing, "*Me Tri-gain-yah.*" They quickly approached the cluster of ram-shackled huts.

Looking around I could see nowhere to hide, and I definitely could not outrun him. Without thinking, I slogged into the water and swam. I moved parallel to the shore, hoping that if he returned, he wouldn't see me. My plan was to come up below the restaurant and run for safety.

Watching, I trembled as I treaded water. Between the roar of the waves, I caught the sounds of music and laughter. The night air was warm, and the water was cool, but not cold. I hesitated to leave the ocean. The fine sand was difficult to walk on and I knew if he was waiting for me, I would not escape. I doubted anyone could hear me scream over the thumping din of the water and music.

I could not see him or Sophie anywhere. I realized that I had abandoned her. Carefully I allowed the current to carry me up to the shore. I lay there, the water breaking over me. Nothing moved. Crawling onto shore, I finally stood and looked around. Then wading through the sand, I scurried up the beach and into the restaurant. Slamming open the door, I almost fell over Sophie, who sat at a round wooden table surrounded by several men. She laughed as she told about our recent ordeal.

I stood there, water dripping onto the rough-hewn wooden floor. Someone handed me a glass of beer and shoved a chair up behind me. Sophie looked approvingly at me, as she continued the tale. I could not believe she had not returned with help, to assist me.

"Pirate Fermin Mundaca!" several voices said at once. Quickly, people crowded around the table as Sophie repeated the story of the man who came out of the sea and attacked me.

"Si! El busce por su Triguena."

"In English!" A tourist moved in and perched on the arm of the chair next to Sophie.

"He looks for his *Triguena*, his brunette lady."

"Me Tri-gain-yah!" Sophie and I repeated; we looked at each other across the table. That was what the man had yelled as he chased Sophie up the beach.

"She was beautiful! Very young, and slim, with large, olive green eyes, that enchanted the men, who all claimed they loved her." The storyteller consulted in Spanish with a few of his companions, then continued the tale. "Mundaca received his architectural training in Spain…" He raised his glass and took a sip before he continued the story. "Mundaca made his fortune as a slave trader and became known as a ruthless pirate of the Caribbean. He fled to the Isle of Mujeres to escape the authorities."

Noting the grumbles, he repeated in English, "The Island of Women. It is believed that the island got its name because many of the pirates kept their wives there. Around 1859 Mundaca took over the island and built a large hacienda and an exquisite garden, which occupied more than 40% of the island."

"Wait!" I thought our orator had misspoke. "You mean in 1959?"

"No," he took a long pull on his beer. "Fermin Mundaca died in 1880."

Sophie sat forward in her chair, raising her hand, "But the man on the beach?"

Several of the Mexican locals murmured; a few crossed themselves. "That was the ghost of Mundaca. He still searches for the Mexican girl, Triguena who stole his heart and possibly his treasure."

Three beers later, we knew the legend of the ghost of Mundaca who came ashore along the Caribbean Coast of Mexico, looking for his runaway love and his lost treasure.

"When the Jaguar screams..." Again, the speaker was interrupted by the other men at the table and he repeated their words in English, "Some claim it is Triguena screaming as he catches her. When we hear the scream, as we did earlier tonight," he looked around the table acknowledging the nods of his companions, "the old pirate walks out of the sea. He attacks women on the shore, demanding that they tell him where he can find Triguena and his treasure. Then he turns and walks straight back into the sea."

I kept insisting on calling the police, but our companions laughed at me and swore that I had been assaulted by the ghost of pirate Mundaca. They claimed the authorities would think I was drunk and lock me up and charge me a stiff fine to release me or worse. Rumors of criminal activity, ignored or even conducted by the police, including kidnapping, sex trading, and extorsion, flew around the table.

"Honestly," I said pulling the neck of my blouse down to reveal a blood smeared collar bone, "I can't believe a ghost can leave bite marks." After years of paranormal investigation, I experienced all manner of bruises and spirit marks, but I never bled.

One of the younger men offered us a ride back to our lodging in his pickup. He claimed he was driving that direction, but I felt he was hoping to have some alone time with Sophie. We both jumped at the offer. Because of my wet clothes I was asked to sit in the bed of the truck. As the vehicle bounced down the road, I heard the screams. They seemed at times just in front of us and other times, just beside.

As we drew near to our campsite, it was apparent that our hut had been toppled and a six-foot hole had been gouged in the center of where it had once stood. As we examined the chaos in the headlights, we could see footprints in the sand. Those of a large cat circled the area and claw marks seemed to tear at the sides of the pit. Then, we noticed a set of large boot prints which led from the wreckage directly to the sea. I shivered, as I watched the man who had assaulted me, walk into the water, then stand and slowly fade from view.

BOOKS BY TERESA CAROL

All Spooked Up
How to Spook Yourself Up

https://www.teresacarol.com/
https://www.doceblant.com/authors/paranormal-investigator-and-intuitive-author-teresa-arol/

Back from the Dead Red

By Marti Melville

"Your leave begins when I say it does, Maltoot!"

The red coat draping over the commanding officer sagged over his shoulders. Three weeks of rain had filled every fiber in the wool he wore—obviously saturated to capacity. The sailor watched as water dripped from the hem of his superior's jacket.

"Aye, sir."

No one dared move. The line of men appropriated to His Majesty's Royal Navy had grown thinner during the voyage. Within days, new recruits would be needed.

The officer began to pace. "Due to the scarcity of rations and personnel aboard this vessel, it will be necessary to restock and re-board. All of you are hereby sequestered into service for another six months, per order from His Majesty, King George."

"But sir …"

In a flash, the captain spun on his heels and faced the men. "Who said that? Who dares to question the king's orders? I'll have him whipped!"

"We haven't seen our homes in more than a year, Capt'n. Surely, we've earned a few hours." The sailor looked at the planks beneath his feet. Indeed, he'd be punished for speaking out of turn—but the crew needed a voice, and it may as well be him, especially as he had no family to speak of.

No one would miss him if he were shot or hanged at the mast—no one except maybe his crewmates.

"What's your name, swabber?"

"Searle, sir. Jacob Searle."

"Well, Jacob Searle—you've just forfeited your first meal onboard. You've also earned a lively jaunt through the gauntlet, which I'm sure your comrades will be more than happy to assist with." Grumbles followed, but no one dared make eye contact with the commanding officer. "Is anyone else interested in expressing an opinion and joining Mr. Searle, as he runs from the cat's scratch?"

"Cat-o-nines? Capt'n!"

"Ah, lovely. We have another volunteer."

Searle glanced at MacBairn and shook his head. "Ye're a solid mate, Danny, but ye're foolish at times. Shut yer trap an' keep yer eyes down." An elbow to the ribs sent the message home, and MacBairn dropped his gaze to the planks as well.

"Anyone else?" The captain eyed the men and waited longer than necessary, relishing in the sight of the men shivering at attention. "Aye, then. Gather what ye must and be back on board no less than forty-five minutes from this moment. Remember, men, deserters will be shot on sight! Dismissed."

Clambering to gather belongings—escape the dock and further scrutiny—the sailors quickly disappeared into harbor pubs and dockside storefronts. Everyone … except Searle and MacBairn, who were stopped short by a polished steel sword. At the other end, the captain sneered.

"Not you two. Your destiny leads you back to the ship."

Both men looked from the blade held in front of them and the ship. There was little aboard that ship that urged them to embark. Each had served long and hard at sea. Insolence had defrauded them, out of the only time on land that they would enjoy for at least another year. Searle whispered an apology to his cohort and slogged his way up the gangplank. Only MacBairn remained where he stood.

"Best join him, swab." The captain glared at him.

But MacBairn stayed in place.

"Danny, he'll run ye through. Up, mate, an' make haste o' it," Searle hollered from the rails. He waved his arms, hoping to snap MacBairn out of a stupid decision.

Just then, a pistol's hammer cocked. The captain shifted his gaze but was unable to see just who held the barrel to his head. MacBairn stared behind at someone on the other end of a firearm.

"Well, now." The voice sounded sultry, female, and lethal. "It appears ye've been less than cordial to yer men, Capt'n."

"I don't know who you are, but I warn you—this misstep will cost you your life at the end of a hangman's noose."

"Oh, I think not. Methinks, it's ye, who've stumbled into a rather foul predicament, *Capt'n*." The sarcasm ran thick as the barrel pressed a little deeper into the captain's scalp.

"You're a bloody pirate and shall hang for this."

Laughter rang out, throaty and fearless. MacBairn watched as the pirate nodded and a young lad scampered behind and up the gangplank.

"Take good care ye don' upset me little brother there, swab, or it'll be yer mate I dispatch first."

Searle watched the lad run across the deck, headed toward the helm. "Aye. Th' lad's safe wit' me."

Within moments, several other pirates had joined him onboard. Each scurried to a pre-assigned task on the ship. The pirate held fast, pistol in place, reminding the captain not to move.

"You'll never get away with this." He finally said, searching the dock for his men. None could be seen; each having taking advantage of the precious leave afforded him. "My men—"

"Ye're men are gone, vanished! Poof!" Again, the pirate laughed. "Should any wish to join me crew, the opportunity will be awarded. As for ye, I've not yet decided what to do with ye, yet."

MacBairn shifted his weight. "I … I'd be willin' to join."

Another chuckle, and MacBairn watched the pirate smile, a toothy, sensuous smile—not fit for a pirate.

"Aye, an' what be yer name, mate?"

"MacBairn … Danny MacBairn." He cleared his throat and glanced at the ship.

"What's yer charge, Danny MacBairn?"

"Carpenter's mate. Powder monkey in battle."

"Well, then, Mr. MacBairn. Methinks ye'd be a fine member o' me crew." A broad grin crossed the pirate's face. "Please board the prize."

He nodded the standard salute and scrambled up the plank, joining Searle at the rails. Skillfully, the pirates on board had prepared the ship for sail. A few had taken up station at the guns. At the end of a long stick held in each man's hand, the amber glow of a taper provided evidence that the guns had been prepped and were ready to fire.

Somewhere behind them, a shot rang out and Searle cried out. He slumped to the rail, nearly falling overboard until MacBairn snatched hold of his collar, dragging him back to the deck. Searle's shoulder oozed through the hole from the slug, staining his shirt a bright crimson. MacBairn clapped both hands over the already displaced extremity that hung grotesquely too low. Searle cried out again.

"Tryin' to stop yer bleedin', mate," MacBairn said, and plastered his handkerchief to the wound. "Someone get rum!"

A pirate wearing a large gold earring and a dirty cerulean head cap handed MacBairn a bottle. He guzzled from it before pouring the rest of its contents into Searle's open mouth. There was little else MacBairn could do until the chirurgeon boarded the ship, so he settled down for the wait. Searle, finally mollified, closed his eyes as the rum took effect.

"Who made that shot?" the pirate with the earring whispered. He peered over the rails, pistol leveled at an invisible shooter on land. "Stay low, lad."

The youth crouched next to Searle, keeping his eyes on MacBairn's efforts to staunch the bleeding. "That's a good lad." MacBairn added, hoping to keep his focus away from the sudden ambush.

"Someone shot at me brother? Fire the guns!" The order came from the dock where the pirate jerked back on the captain, still holding a pistol to his head. "Level the bloody curs! This town's unfit to stand. I'll not have me crew fired upon by cowardly landlubbers, hidin' themselves in balustrades an' women's skirts!"

Another shot rang out, this time splintering the dock where they stood. Within moments, the crowded streets had emptied. Bystanders peeked out through corners and cracks in shuttered windows as the pirates returned fire.

Just then, a cannon erupted from the side of the ship, spewing smoke and fire, followed by a cannonball that blasted into the front of a tavern. Folks hidden within screamed at the same time body parts and wood exploded from the building. Those untouched, ran out of the flaming structure, pistols and blades held high in defense. Another blast leveled the neighboring cooperage, filling the air with thick black smoke.

The pirate dragged the captain backward, pulling him toward the gangplank. A loud whistle sounded, and several additional pirates sprinted across the cobblestone road and up the gangplank. Spilling onto the dock, a handful of sailors approached, then stopped short as they caught sight of their captain, pistol to scalp, in the hands of a pirate.

"Choose gents—join me crew or perish." The pirate urged the captain onto the gangplank.

Just then, an explosion sounded from the fort portside, and the water heaved itself over the side of the ship.

"They're firing on us!" one of the pirates shouted the obvious.

The crew scrambled to light the next big gun while three men pulled it into position, ready to return fire.

"Quickly men, as it seems yer own beloved Cagway town seeks to dispatch ye!" The pirate jerked the captain on deck then turned to face the crew. "Make sail, ho!"

"Hard over!" came the reply from the helm.

Another blast from the fort sent sea spray across the deck and the ship heaved. Several of the pirates lost their footing, but quickly recovered, dropping the sails and securing them. The ship suddenly lifted, pulling against its anchorage. Again, the fort fired upon them.

"We cut an' run. Haste men!"

Below, the cluster of befuddled sailors skittered up the gangplank shouting, "Join! We join!" as they boarded.

A pirate drew out his cutlass, severing the mooring lines, and the ship broke free from its quay. Just then, the wind caught the sails and the ship lurched. Saltwater sprayed the bow as the sea welcomed the ship back to open water. Cheers sounded and the pirates raised their weapons as the Jamaica's final effort to foil the pirates fell short, cannonballs landing haplessly in the distance.

Stepping forward, the pirate shoved the British captain forward. "Aye, mate. It appears ye've lost yer ship. What's left o' yer crew have elected me as their new capt'n."

"You're a rotten scallywag! Bloody scum!" the captain said and spit.

The pirate sighed. "It seems, ye're unhappy here, and we've no need o' that. Aye?"

Gathered around them, the newly formed crew voiced their agreement. The pirate glanced at the men and smiled.

"Traitors!" the captain screamed at the men. "You'll all hang!"

"I think we've grown tired of yer threats sir." The pirate turned and walked to the foc's'le and faced them all. In a single swipe, the pirate pulled the tri-corn from atop a crown of auburn hair. Ringlets fell nearly to her waist and the scent of cinnamon followed. She threw back her head and chortled, the same throaty, sensuous laugh as before, then lowered her eyes and glared. "Feed him to the sharks!"

Several stepped forward, dragging the captain to the rails. Though he thrashed, the pirates had no issue subduing him. Within moments, a resounding splash sounded as the captain's body hit the water. His screams sounded for only a few minutes before the current pulled at his waterlogged coat and doused him to silence.

Searle stared at the woman, mesmerized as much by her tenacity as by her beauty. Even MacBairn had propped himself up to gaze at her. "Who is she?" he whispered. Searle gave no answer but stared dumbfounded.

"What do they call you, Madame?" MacBairn's voice sounded weak. Still, he voiced the question most were afraid to ask.

She laughed again and shook her curls. Then, smiling at MacBairn, dropped her pistol into the belt at her hip and rested her hands on her hips. Staring at him for a moment, she cocked her head and responded, "As ye're injured, and likely not of full faculties, I'll forgive yer ignorance this time. Be mindful ye don't forget me, sailor."

"MacBairn," he said absently.

"Mister MacBairn, it be then." She paused for effect. "Indeed, many do call me 'Madame,' though I'm not a lady, as ye note. I'm known as 'pirate' or 'scallywag,' mostly as Madame Jaquotte Delahaye ." She paused again and tossed her head.

"Madame Delahaye." The crew echoed.

"Aye. So what do we call ye?" Searle spoke this time and she shook her head. Cinnamon scented the air again and the men gasped as they stared, slack-jawed, at the mesmerizing beauty in command. Moments later, she answered them with a name they'd likely never forget…

"Back from the Dead, Red."

BOOKS BY MARTI MELVILLE

The Déjà vu Chronicles:
Midnight Omen (book 1)
Silver Moon (book 2)
Onyx Rising (book 3)
Cutthroat's Omen: A Crimson Dawn (book 4)

Grandma BallyHuHu and the Mystical Coin
Grandma BallyHuHu and the Sparkly TuTu
Grandma BallyHuHu and the Missing Pandas

https://martimelville.com/
https://www.doceblant.com/authors/marti-melville/

Lost Among Waves

By P. J. Roscoe

Elsa lit a match and held it to the wick of the small, white candle. Almost immediately the flame came to life and lit up her face in the growing darkness. She let go of the breath she had been holding and immediately went about lighting the rest of the candles in the small, dark room. There were nine candles scattered around in total and by the time she had finished, a soft, romantic glow emanated from everywhere and she smiled to herself, despite the fluttering of apprehension that beat against her insides.

She gazed around at the dark oak wood paneling, finishing on the solid oak door that she knew led outside where the wind blew and the rain pelted against the earth. She was soddened after her run from the car, parked half a mile further down the lane due to there being no access via the road. She quickly took off her dripping coat and reached for a small hand towel she had placed in her overnight bag, just before leaving for this adventure.

Hair drying and skin glowing from the biting cold, she turned her attention to the fireplace. As promised, it was laid ready for lighting and she did with haste. The old wood caught immediately, and warmth filled the air. Inviting, was a word that sprung to mind, if she could ignore where she actually was.

Sitting like a beacon atop a high cliff, 'Smugglers Way inn' was a fifteenth century tavern that described exactly what it once was. Beyond the pub's garden, steps led down to a small cove where a large cave could be found, with the entrance half hidden between two rocks. The cave goes back quite far into the cliffs and they say a tunnel once led up to the inn, though that has long since been lost from land falls. For centuries, men would use this cave and inn to hide their goods from the king's men and it is said, up until fairly recently, the caves were still in use by persons unknown, though the loot hadn't changed much. Tobacco and alcohol were still the bounty of smugglers.

Elsa sighed loudly and pushed aside her doubts of what she was about to do. The inn had been abandoned these last five years as the cliff edge slowly drew closer due to erosion. The owners had been offering the inn to local ghost chasers in a last-ditch attempt to claim some money back on a bad investment. Groups from all over England and beyond had taken them up on the offer. Most never remained the full night and none ever came back for a second visit. It was during one of her Friday night pub crawls that she'd met two men from the last ghost hunt held there a month before. They and six others had paid to stay the night. They'd lasted three hours before fleeing. Describing the old inn, Elsa was hooked and contacted the owner the next day.

Now two weeks later. Instead of throwing back the fine ales with her friends, she was here, alone and waiting. The owner, Mr. Jackson hadn't been impressed that it was only one, but Elsa had paid him double to be sure of entry. Greed won, as it always did, though he did have the decency to look troubled by it.

'Are you sure you want to stay there alone? Perhaps pay me for an hour or so…?'

Elsa reassured him she was fine and had done this many times before. This was true. No ghost chaser searching for a cheap thrill. Elsa was a medium. She had travelled the country searching for ghosts and spirits to talk to and help move on once their problem was sorted, but this was different. Having never been to the inn before in all her thirty- seven years, as soon as she heard the description, she knew it to be the one. Having run from the car, she had stood before the inn as the night slowly claimed the day and she had almost wept on seeing that she'd been right. It was here she would finally find him. The man who haunted her every night. He would call to her and she would run to him. His arms embracing her tightly, declaring he would never set her free again and she would wake, whimpering as tears fell down her cheeks.

Rubbing her hands together to help the warmth circulate, she laid another log on the growing fire, inhaling the smoky scent of apple wood. A hard chair next to the fire was the only furniture in the room but she ignored it and went to sit in the window seat so that she could look out at the storm.

Glancing at her watch, she yawned. Nine thirty. According to the two men of the ghost group, they had fled just after midnight, having set up cameras, tape recorders and trigger objects around the inn. Exhaustion pulled at her. It had been a long drive to reach here before sundown. Rubbing her eyes, she considered looking around the rest of the inn. Besides this room, there was another snug where the large bar could be found, a small area used as the restaurant, toilets and the kitchen. Upstairs was the two bed-roomed flat for the owners. Elsa found her large torch and picked up one of the candles. She walked towards the closed door and stopped to listen. Hearing nothing and feeling nothing, she gently opened it and headed for the bathrooms. Once refreshed, she wandered into the smaller snug. The room felt oppressive and cold. Without rushing, Elsa looked behind the empty bar, before walking out into the hallway that separated the two rooms.

She immediately stopped to listen. Movement from within the room where she had lit the fire caused her to freeze. She had locked the front door, yet every ounce of her being told her there was someone waiting for her.

'Hello?'

Nothing. Yet it felt as though someone held their own breath, waiting. Listening.

'Hello? Captain? Is that you?'

She listened hard, but no sound came from within. There was nothing for it, she'd have to go in and confront him. Elsa walked slowly, listening with every step. Reaching the half open door, she pushed it open. He stood half turned away from her. He gazed down at the fire and as she walked further into the room, she saw such sadness, her own trepidation dissolved in a heartbeat. 'It is you…?'

He turned then at the sound of her voice and she knew without any doubt that she knew him. Although in this semi darkness, his eyes seemed black, she knew they were a deep green. His mouth full and promising. His auburn hair fell in waves from beneath his brown tricorn hat to his muscular shoulders and his hands that held such power and force when dealing with men, but with her, he was gentle and loving. His touch lit a spark without fail.

'Do you know me then?' His voice, deep and velvet, questioning yet he held a slight amusement.

Elsa could not tear her gaze away. 'I…I think I do. But how…When…?'

Ignoring her questions, the man stepped closer. Reaching out, he touched her cheek and smiled. 'Will you come with me?'

Elsa closed her eyes. The cancer that had taken hold years before had been the ticking clock that pushed her onwards to find the answers from the dead. She'd known her time was limited. His touch was cool and familiar. She opened her eyes and smiled. 'Is it time?'

'Aye lass, it is. I have waited here for you, as promised, all those centuries ago before they could hang me. The men are waiting in the ship below. Will you come?' He repeated.

Elsa stared into her husband's eyes and remembered everything. They had been betrayed to the crown. Having made a run for it, here; to the caves where the king's men had dragged them apart on finding the tunnel blocked with nowhere to run. Laughing, they had made her watch as they hung her husband, the notorious pirate, Captain Nicholas Swan, before sending her to London where she died in prison. Elsa moved into his arms, closed her eyes in bliss, as the breath left her, remembering his last words to her as they kissed for the last time before being torn apart. 'I will wait here for you my love, always.'

Elsa opened her eyes and found herself outside. The wind no longer howled, and the rain no longer fell. The sky was red as the sun set beyond the horizon and she looked down from the top of the cliffs and smiled on seeing the ship. Nicholas squeezed her hand before lifting it to his lips. 'Forever my love. Forever…'

BOOKS BY P.J. ROSCOE

Echoes
Diary of Margery Blake

https://www.doceblant.com/p-j-roscoe/
http://www.pjroscoe.co.uk/

And Other Ships Flee

(A SEA SHANTY)

The dead lay 'bout below the field
Huzzah!
Those lying o'er grassy fields doth rot
Huzzah!
But by me hand their Maker sought
Huzzah!
Their souls do rest in peace.
Huzzah!
Let out the sails and mind the rails
We go to sea as other ships flee
And hoist the colors, Ho!
Huzzah!

An excerpt From: *Onyx Rising* (book 3 – *The Déjà vu Chronicles*) by Marti Melville

https://martimelville.com/
https://www.doceblant.com/authors/marti-melville/

The Stupidest Mistake Ever Made by Pirates

BY DAVID K. BRYANT

You can imagine the conversation between the pirates.

"Ah ha," says one. "Look what we've got here. A Roman senator. We can hold him as a hostage."

"Oh yes," enthuses Pirate Number 2. "We'll get a packet in ransom."

Never has any pirate crew made a bigger mistake.

They didn't know it but their target was Gaius Julius Caesar, who would go on to conquer Gaul (modern France), bring Egypt under Roman control, take the Romans into England for the first time, and overcome his rivals to become dictator of Rome and all the states it controlled. Not only that, he invented the 365-day calendar.

One of the most accomplished men in history was not going to be intimidated by the ragtag bunch of buccaneers who waylaid his ship on the Aegean Sea while he was on his way to learn rhetoric in Rhodes.

"So what do you want?" asked Caesar.

"I reckon we'll get twenty talents of silver for you," boasted the pirate chief.

Well, the only thing that overcame Gaius Julius at that point was laughter. He creased up, wiped the tears of hilarity from his eyes and mocked: "Twenty talents. By Jupiter, you're dumb. You just don't realize who you've captured. Let me give you a tip—ask for fifty. You'll easily make that."

Okay, I've paraphrased, but that's pretty much the way it went.

The record of this historical treat from the year 75 BC is provided by the Greek author Plutarch in his *Life of Julius Caesar*. There is also reference to it by the Roman writer Tacitus.

Up until the misbegotten abduction of Caesar, the Romans had turned a blind eye to the pirates in return for a steady supply of slaves. The arrangement ensured that piracy became a burgeoning profession and the Mediterranean was infested with this early version of privateers.

Plutarch tells us that the misguided kidnappers were from Cilicia, now part of southern Turkey and Cyprus. They were regarded as the most blood-thirsty villains in the world. So they must have been shocked at Caesar's nonchalant reaction to them.

He didn't stop at acting as a financial advisor. While his agents were away raising the money, Caesar began bossing the pirates around.

If they kept him awake with their chatter, Caesar would send a "shut up" message.

It got to the point where the man who would later prove his tactical abilities in many other ways became more like the pirate captain than their captive.

He joined in their games and exercises and even tried to improve their education by writing poems and speeches which he read out to them. Now, anybody who has read Caesar's turgid and self-serving memoirs will know what a torture that must have been for the wretched fortune-hunters. If they failed to admire his work, he told them straight that they were "illiterate savages".

The Stupidest Mistake Ever Made by Pirates

What a persona that man must have had. You can see why prominent Romans later feared he had ambitions of becoming their king and he was bumped off as a result.

Anyway, back to the "blood-thirsty" pirates. "I'll have you executed," Caesar warned them.

"Is he simple, immature or a joker?" they asked each other about their 25-year-old guest.

The farce went on for thirty-eight days. Then, to what must have been the enormous relief of all concerned, the ransom arrived.

Caesar put a fleet and an armed force together then went back—to find his dim ex-captors languishing around in the same spot. This time they were taken prisoner and all their property, including the 50 talents, was confiscated as spoils of war.

Next, the intrepid Caesar went to the governor of Asia and said: "This is your jurisdiction. Sit in judgment on these riff-raff."

The governor procrastinated. He had his eye on the treasure taken from the pirates.

So Caesar did a vigilante act. He unlocked the jail, marched out the pirates and crucified the lot of them. But he showed some leniency—he had their throats cut first. You can imagine him mocking: "I gave you fair warning."

Nine years later, the Mediterranean piracy problem was solved by Pompey the Great who took out a massive fleet and defeated the pirates, taking many of them into custody. But he did not serve up the same retribution as Caesar, instead setting up the Cilicians with plots of land and transforming them into farmers.

The ghosts of those scoundrels put on the cross by Caesar must have thought: "If only we'd waited…"

Caesar and Pompey were allies at that time and Caesar supported Pompey's expedition against the buccaneers. Later, however, these two Roman titans became rivals as the Roman republic crumbled and the state moved inexorably towards being an autocracy.

After a battle won by Caesar, Pompey fled to Egypt and was betrayed by those who thought they would curry favor with Caesar. Pompey's head was delivered to Caesar but, far from being pleased at the extermination of his competitor, Caesar was distressed that such a prominent Roman had met an ignominious end.

It left the field clear for Caesar to pursue his own ambition which, most likely, was to become a monarch. He probably displayed the same loftiness with his peers as he had done with the unfortunate pirates.

Those who wanted Rome to cling on to its fading status as a republic had their say on the Ides of March when they murdered Caesar.

After more civil wars, Rome became an empire with Caesar's adopted son, Augustus, becoming the first emperor. The name Caesar was to live on, being inherited by the subsequent emperors. It survives to this day. Among the derivatives are czar and kaiser.

But the names of the pirates who thought they were kidnapping some run-of-the-mill senator have long been forgotten.

BOOKS BY DAVID K. BRYANT

Beyond the Last Hill
Dust of Cannae

https://www.doceblant.com/david-k-bryant/

Avast

BY REN CUMMINS

The crew was silent as the *Monkey's Duffle* eased its way towards port. The waves and the creaking ropes offered a rhythmic orchestration to the noises that came from the high sails as the winds brought them back home. At least, "home" was a word only few on the ship could comfortably use for describing the sole town on Uphoria's core island. They came back here every few months when necessary, and never stayed long, just as they did with all the island communities on their cyclical route across the sea. But, after all, it was to be expected, based upon their collective profession: *piracy*. This town, now, was thought of less than a home and more a victim of their pirating activities.

All the ship hands—all pirates, either by trade or association—had begun their journey on or around the island, sure enough, but time had eventually seen them onto the deck of this or one of the other privateering vessels that frequented the region.

Four-Eyed Robert had maintained the helm the last few hours, steering the ship past the tall columns of natural stone that the local townspeople called the *Shadow's Fangs*. Though treacherous, they also marked the relatively safest entrance into Nikada bay, where the main docks for Uphoria port had been constructed. *How long ago had they been built? They'd been old, long before the arrival of any of them; one of the many mysteries about this place*, he shrugged.

The men were already climbing the rigging to draw up the sails; inertia and tide would carry the ship the rest of the way into the harbor. The first thing, though, was the striking of their false colors—Jimmy Doubloons was already taking down their normal flag, the bleach-white skull on a field of black that marked them for their truer natures. He'd replace it with one of their other flags, usually one that they'd taken in plunder. Robert hissed up at him as he noticed Jimmy was tying the flag off upside-down. It took Jimmy a full minute to realize his error and he scrambled to correct it, doing so only a moment before their ship would be in full view of the harbor master's perimeter station. Sure enough, he'd barely had time to hunker down before a voice called out to them.

Trouble with making port after nightfall is that they always suspect us for pirates, Robert thought. *Which would only be insulting if it weren't also the truth*. It was a true "catch-22," he observed, for if they cast ashore during the day, then of course their nature would be obvious. Thus, the only feasible alternative was a quick foray into the harbor after nightfall, with the intention of being gone before sunrise. Generally, it was effective. Generally.

They lashed up at the docks, three of the men dropping down to tie off the *Monkey's Duffle*'s main lines. Robert tied off the wheel and nearly tripped over a loose rope on his way back to the main deck. He had to pause and clean his glasses; they'd picked up a bit of spray and had gone fuzzy without him even having noticed. His glasses were in bad shape; he'd had them ever since he could remember. There weren't any folks who could repair something so delicate here; so he had to make do with the options remaining available to him. As a result, the glasses looked more like a pair of goggles than how they'd been when he'd arrived here. Now, a hardened leather band and a softer, pliable strap kept them affixed to his head. They were as secure as they were going to be, but they still seemed to attract dirt and sea salt like it was mating season.

Without them, he was effectively blind; he couldn't see much further than his hands without squinting, and from bow to stern he was useless. Still, he was the ship's captain, potential blindness or otherwise. His background made him the most tactical of the crew. After a pair of near-defeats, at the hands of some of the other pirate clans proved the end for the Duffel's former Captain; the crew turned to him to lead. It'd been…years, he calculated, though it was nigh-impossible to have a true appreciation for the passage of time. Between the life as a pirate captain and the odd way time seemed to flow here in Uphoria, Robert figured that he'd been here somewhere between fifteen days and seven years. Give or take a decade.

He tried to track this as best as possible by refusing to cut his hair. He'd grown it out once in college—back when it was apparently cool to do so—and it had taken a year to get his hair to reach his shoulder blades. It was now drawn back into a thick braid that reached down to his belt, adorned with random coins and baubles they'd acquired along their way.

College, he thought, his forehead scrunching up beneath his bandana. *Where did that come from? When did I go to college?* Strange thoughts occurred to him from time to time, without sense or reason as to their origins. He used to have a recurring dream about sitting in front of a dull mirror, filled with mystical lights and words and strange images. He would use the mirror to obtain all knowledge, simply by asking the proper questions; or transport his mind into faraway worlds where he lived a thousand mysterious lives. In these other worlds, he was a soldier, a practitioner of dark arts, a god, a demon. Wasn't one of those dreams about him being a pirate? He paused, one foot on the deck and one on the bottom step that led astern towards the wheel.

What if the dream is real? His mind spun. *What if my dreams are the reality, and this is the dream? What if...* A hand clapped him on the shoulders, jarring him from his thoughts.

"Ho, Cap'n," came the voice beside him.

Robert's jaw jerked upwards in a gruff nod. "Gadrick," he said.

Gadrick No-Nails was his Master Gunner, so named for an unfortunate incident in the early part of his career involving cleaning up a barrel of spilled gunpowder and someone else's brilliant idea of daring Gadrick to run his dirty hands over an open flame. An otherwise reliable enough man, prone to drink too much and talk too loudly, but few could match his precision with the heavy guns. Then again, Gadrick was the perennial pirate. When Robert was given the wheel, Gadrick was at that time his most vocal opponent. But with the crew behind Four-Eyed Robert, Gadrick had nothing else to do but toe the line.

"Catch ya dreamin'?"

Sliding the glasses back over his eyes, Robert allowed himself a brief chuckle. "Just looking forward to an evening in town, is all," he lied.

Gadrick's echoed laugh trailed off as his gaze dropped to the captain's belt. "Goin' ashore a bit…naked, ain'tcha?"

Robert's hands went to his belt and he cursed silently. He'd left his bandolier and weapons belt back in his cabin. The rest of the crew heard Gadrick's comment and paused, regarding them both. Robert jerked a thumb towards the town. "Won't be long, you and the men run on ahead," he ordered. "Tyler Tats," he said in a soft voice which still carried well across the deck, "you keep a boarding crew on hand and fire off a flare if there's trouble."

"Aye," Tyler replied, pulling a small contingent of crew aside to defend the ship. Gadrick pushed through the throng at the plank and led a crew of three dozen along the pontoon-supported dock and up towards the town. It was the best part of the town; the depth of the harbor allowed for even the tall ships to pull in fairly close, even at low tide.

Provided the men kept their cool, they could be back on the ship and heading for open waters before the watch was alerted. And even if not, Tyler and his team—making up just less than half the total crew—would be enough to handle the ship. Either way, speed and silence were key. With them, the whole plan was smooth.

Then again, Robert thought as he moved quickly back to his cabin, *how many times has that happened?*

Slipping the bandolier over his shoulder and quickly strapping on his second belt, he double-checked his rapier and pistol, weighed his powder horn and was already loading a round as he emerged onto the deck. "Keep the engine warm," he said to Tyler and his men, even though their confused expressions made more sense to him than the statement.

Engine? He wondered, shaking his head. *No more rum tonight for this pirate*, he decided.

He wasn't even to the end of the dock before he came across the first body. By the look of him, he was little more than an unfortunate victim of location and bad timing; his clothing didn't even mark him for a constable, and he was probably just walking the docks for spare goods left abandoned by the day's traders. Robert raised him up into a sitting position against one of the raised pilings, arranging his hands to make it appear as if he was simply sleeping. *At least they didn't shoot him*, Robert grimaced. *That would've cut this whole trip really short.*

It had taken a while, but he'd managed to convince his crew to focus their search and plunder missions. Time was, their escapades resulted mostly in murder and raping, and over time, he thankfully was able to replace that segment of the crew due to being hoisted on their own petards. Now, however, they worked in particular teams, all fixed to acquire specific materials; food, tradable goods, weapons and rum. The categories had been easy enough to insist upon, though the prioritization had taken a while. He had been firm on one other rule: *no raping*. There were plenty of other pirate crews out on the water that gave them all a deservedly poor reputation, but Robert was resolved to giving them at least one less reason to be feared and hated.

It was doubtful that pirates would ever have a favorable image in the eyes of the citizens of Uphoria, but perhaps in time…he shook his head. *Get your game face on*, Robert, he told himself. *We're in play now.*

He moved quickly and quietly through the streets, his right hand holding his flintlock pistol up and just at the lower edge of his vision. For some reason, it just felt more comfortable to have it right there as they went ashore on their scavenging missions.

The door to the harbormaster's office was opened; Robert clucked his tongue twice, and, after a pause heard three in return. Satisfied with the countersign, he peered inside to see two of his men hefting the lockbox. A muffled bit of jingling could be heard coming from inside the sealed container and judging by the greedy smiles on his men's faces, it was clearly heavy with loot.

"Good job," he whispered as he stepped aside to let them pass. A third man accompanied them, pistols out and at the ready. They exchanged nods as they moved past him towards the docks, walking as swiftly as they dared.

Across the street, a pair of men had just opened a locked doorway to the smithy. Robert was of half a mind to join them; the hilt on his own rapier was getting loose and he could do with a fresh one. He was sure he'd mentioned it to the crew earlier, though, so he chose to hope they'd remember. If in fact they came across something that would be to his liking, at any rate.

Past the next cross street, he found the third team, who had broken into one of the storehouses for the marketplace; a typically secured location. Robert walked to the doors and sounded off again and waited for the agreed-upon response. A small smear of blood remained on the doorjamb, evoking a brief frown on the Captain's face. Well inside the room, he could see a pair of bare feet emerging from behind a desk, the boots already plucked from the poor bastard's still-cooling corpse.

Though he wasn't universally opposed to violence, Captain Robert preferred as low a body count as possible. Sometimes, however, it was simply out of his hands. *May they return to life in a better place*, he thought.

As the three men that comprised the third team stepped back into the room with a series of crate in their hands, the second man glanced ashamedly at the corpse on the floor. "Beggin' yer pardon, Cap'n, but he'd've raised the alarm had we letten him live," he said soberly.

Robert nodded slowly. "You did fine, gentlemen, it's no slight on your honor. Move on, now, quiet as you like."

As the men obeyed, the Captain stood a moment longer over the body. Was this to be his life, then? Pillaging? Murdering? Scavenging at the end of a cutlass for the sustenance his crew required?

Distorted memories of his childhood passed his thoughts; the insistence and enforced premise that pirates were evil, that they stood in rank defiance to the laws and order which kept society moving, that piracy of all manner was wrong. He had to admit that statements like that made his blood boil furiously. *Who are they to say I am evil? Do not some laws require by their nature an act of defiance?*

But who says such things? The church, he answered himself, *and the government*. He spat on the floor, as if trying to purge a sudden bitterness from his mouth. *Well, I don't fear the government or the church. They should fear —*

A woman's scream two buildings away cut through his musings like a gunshot. He ran in pursuit of the sound, even as he could hear voices stirring in the buildings around him.

Ahead of him stood one of the town's three pubs, its door slightly ajar. *It's Gadrick*, he realized, knowing full well that Gadrick always positioned himself to claim the rum on their inland forays. *Damn fool is going to get us killed.*

The clatter of crockery greeted him at the doorway. He looked quickly inside to see two of Gadrick's men moving towards the door, carrying one large barrel each. Robert stepped aside, pushing the door open for them.

"Hurry back, lads," he muttered, wincing in response to additional cries coming from the next room. He quietly closed the door behind them, and walked towards the source of the cries, which by now were coming in a horrifyingly steady rhythm. Robert moved across the wooden floor, taking each step in time to the cries, just in case a wayward creak might give his presence away.

Robert stood to one side of the arched doorway that led to the kitchen, glancing quickly into the room to take inventory of the situation. It didn't take much.

Gadrick had thrown some poor young woman over the far table in the kitchen and hitched up her skirts. He had both her hands in one of his and was holding her by the waist, struggling in his furious efforts to assault her.

Robert double-checked the flintlock's frizzen; the powder was still ready to fire. Stepping out into the doorway, he held the pistol up and directed it towards his Master Gunner. "Gadrick!" He cocked the pistol, letting the distinct *click-clack* of the mechanism punctuate the man's name.

Gadrick stopped, standing upright but still holding the struggling woman down. Without even glancing back over his shoulder, he nodded.

"Thought I'd had another few minutes to meself," the man said. "T'isn't polite to interrupt a man's pleasure."

"Less polite to disobey your Captain," Robert replied. "Step away from her and let her go, and maybe you'll only spend a week in the brig."

Turning his head slightly to look back at his Captain, Gadrick shrugged. "Jus' havin' a bit of fun, there, Cappy, jus' me an' m'girl, here, ain't that right, luv?"

But Robert could see enough in the sobs and the tear-streaked face to know the lie for what it was. Worse, he knew Gadrick well enough already to be dubious of the man ever having a willing partner.

"I said to let her go. Now."

The other man slowly stepped back from the girl, and she fell over onto the floor in her desperation to get away. Gadrick eyed her briefly, the faintest flash of vitriol passing his features before looking back up to his Captain. He pointed downwards, indicating his breeches that remained about his ankles. "One tic," he mumbled. "Jus' gonna tuck meself back in."

Meanwhile, the girl had managed to stand up again and was rushing to stand behind Robert.

"Make it quick."

With a curt nod of his greasy head, Gadrick disappeared briefly behind the table. He came back up a moment later with a pistol in hand.

Robert drew back on the trigger; felt the powerful kick of the black powder's explosion in the chamber as the room filled with smoke and thunder as the shot rang out. His ears just barely picked up the sound of Gadrick's own gun cocking, and as soon as he fired, he used the burst of smoke to conceal him as he turned and pulled the girl to the right side of the doorway.

Sure enough, a second shot rang out only a moment later, the load bursting through a window on the other side of the room.

His ears were still ringing from the double discharges, probably would be for an hour or so. But he was already loading his second shot and could hear Gadrick doing the same.

"This won't play out well," he shouted. Whistles were sounding in the streets outside. "Hear that? Minutes more, and we'll be up to our poop decks in the brass!"

"Y'think I likes this?" Gadrick's voice bellowed back at him from behind the kitchen table. "Between the moldy potato bread, the foot rot and those damned Losties, y'think this is a life any of us wanted?"

Robert sighed. His Master Gunner did have a good point. "Doesn't mean you can just take what you like, Gadrick. These are people, too!"

"They're damn sheep!" the other man yelled back. "*They make it, we take it*—that's the way it is, there's no other way of it."

Robert could hear the volume and tone of Gadrick's voice changing; he was moving around in there. *Going to make it hard to get a shot off if I don't know where he is*, he thought ruefully. "I only had two rules, you shitheel—*beg pardon, ma'am*—no killing lest you had to, and no raping. None!"

He peered around the corner just in time to take a glancing blow across the face from a cast iron frying pan. He could hear something crunching under the impact, and distantly felt the floor rise up to strike him across the back of his head. A warm rush of blood covered his eyes and face. It felt for a moment like his skull was opened to the world.

A boot came down hard on his shoulder, pushing him all the way prone. Blood was in his eyes, and he couldn't see; but he felt death's hand reaching through the night-time ocean breezes and the smell of old beer.

Didn't someone tell me I'd die on the floor of a bar? I guess I'll have to let them know they were right.

"Last time you give me an order, Four Eyes," the man above him chuckled. Then a hammer was drawn back, and a final explosion tore open Robert's chest and blasted him into nothingness.

…He tapped the X button on his controller and waited through the uploading screen. His fingers twitched. So what if he'd been playing all evening, he could always call in sick tomorrow. It's not like they had a shortage of IT support personnel or anything.

The page flashed, concussions and flak from the opposing assault shaking the controller and buzzing in his headphones. He held down the jump button and jerked his thumb to the left, moving his character behind a section of wall that was still standing. "I need some cover fire over here!" he barked into the mouthpiece.

Moments later, another of the gold team stood out from their bunker in full auto, laying out a swatch of destruction while another of their team launched a round of grenades into the enemies' position.

He laughed, getting his character back on his feet and running to the location where the opposing flag would re-spawn.

"We got you, Captain!" the voices cheered over the speakers. "Grab it and haul ass!"

The flag appeared just as he entered the room, but so did one of the Green team, wielding a military shotgun.

The spray went wide, only dropping his shield bar by a fraction; he rolled low and came up beside his opponent, raking him across the temple with the butt of his rifle. As the enemy stumbled, Robert drew his service knife and pulled the blade quickly across the man's neck.

The screen flashed and the body dropped to the floor. Robert paused just long enough to *teabag* the poor schmuck before holstering the knife and picking up the flag.

"Coming out!" he yelled into the mike. "Get ready!"

He made it five running steps, and the laughter was still fresh on his lips when the ground erupted beneath him.

Mother fu… They've got a tank!

<respawn in five…four…three…two…one…>

"Hold still, young man, hold still."

Arms held him down, and a woman's voice spoke to him in soothing tones. "Relax, there you go, just relax, and you'll be fine."

Robert tried to breathe, but it was a struggle, as if someone were sitting across his chest.

"Breathe easy, lad," another voice said, encouragingly. "Have you patched up presently."

He at last was able to pry his eyes open—they were gummed up and stung from the sticky blood which still coated them, and the world around him was blurry.

My glasses! He realized. He tried to lift his arms, but they were held fast to his sides.

"My...," he said aloud, but he could only take short breaths before he could continue, "...glasses."

A large fuzzy person-shaped outline whose hands were on Robert's chest turned an indistinct blob of a head to another fuzzy outline that knelt beside him. "It's okay, you can let go of his arm, this young man understands that we're helping him."

The other person released their grip on Robert's left hand, and he lifted it with some discomfort to his face. The goggles were still there, but the lenses were gone; only a few jagged bits remained in the frames, and he winced as one of them drew blood.

"Okay, Miriam, why don't you get those off the boy's face, he's only going to cut himself up again."

A third figure—Miriam, he supposed—reached down and carefully slid the goggles off his head, her fingers returning to his face to gingerly pluck away the lingering bits of glass and to daub away the blood with a wet cloth.

He blinked, his eyes straining to peer through the haze even as his mind struggled to resist the realization that, at long last, he was blind, here. "How...long?"

"How long you been shot?" the older, male voice asked. "Not five, six minutes since we got here. Saw your friend scamper off, looked only a bit better off than you."

"Trail of blood leads off towards the docks," another voice offered.

"And fore you think of it," the first man cautioned, giving Robert's chest a gentle pat that sent an ache down both arms, "I think you'll agree that you're in no shape to follow. Best take it as a loss and be grateful; if he'd been a steadier shot, you wouldn't be here no how."

Steadier shot? Gadrick? But he…never missed. It didn't make sense. Nothing made sense. *I should be dead. Why am I not dead?* The word "respawn" fluttered back to his mind, but he ignored it until it went away. As he lay there, he could hear the cannon fire from the harbor towers, and the return fire from the *Monkey's Duffle*. He'd lived with those cannons for so long now, they were like the cries of his children. With each shot launched from the harbor's big guns, he paused, listening intently for the associated splash.

The old man was a bit clearer in focus now. "So, lad, tell me this: suren, you're anxious about them cannon shots aimed at that vessel making her way out t'sea, I can see it plain enough on your face. But," he added, drawing his face nearer to Robert's, "are you hoping she's sunk, or are you hoping she's free?"

Robert took a slow breath. "I…I don't know," he confessed.

The old man nodded, patting Robert, former Captain of the pirate ship *Monkey's Duffle* on the shoulder. "You and me both."

Full recovery took a few weeks, but eventually Robert was back again among the living, and got commissioned into the harbormaster's duty roster. His experience as Captain proved invaluable to helping the town set up a more rigid defensive plan for the town.

At first, he'd felt conflicted by the requests they made of him; but logic prevailed. After all, they'd saved his life, and, as it turned out, they were a good people: hard working, friendly and generous. The reluctance he'd initially felt—as if he'd been betraying his ship and crew—were quickly replaced by the guilt for his years of pillaging and resultant fear he'd no doubt had a hand with instilling into the hearts of its townspeople. And each night, with the setting of the sun, he found himself looking out into the dying embers of each period of daylight, for any sign of top sails coming their way.

Without his glasses, he'd feared he would be effectively useless, but as it turned out the smith—a jovial behemoth of a man, named Daniels—was also quite adept at fashioning glass into the lenses they used for their spyglasses. By the time Robert was back on his feet, Daniels had already created a replacement pair for him. The material was a bit imperfect, and his right lens wasn't quite strong enough, giving him headaches if he used them for too long. But headaches were a fair sight better than functional blindness, and a price he was all too willing to pay.

Additionally, the same Miriam who had stood by him while the old doctor had treated him remained beside Robert through his convalescence, caring for him until he was fully restored. When their friendship turned into something more was a hard question to answer, however. They had struck up a romance during his time under her care, and their relationship already had the town abuzz with talk of a spring wedding.

And so it was that when the *Monkey's Duffle* returned to port, her former Captain Robert found that he now had something worth fighting for.

He had been leaving Miriam's house and his lips were still tingling with the memory of her kisses when movement from the bay drew his eyes. Robert had to cover his right eye so he could get a decent look at it and caught just a faint impression of a dark shadow within the blackness that hung over the water.

"Damned fools," he shook his head as he broke into a run towards the harbor guard terminal. The ship had just passed the *Shadow's Fangs*, giving them perhaps five minutes until they reached the docks. *Still plenty of time.* He smiled, skidding to a stop inside the barracks.

One of the watchmen spun about as he entered. "Captain Robert!" he exclaimed. "It's a ship, sure enough—is it the Duffle?"

He'd initially resisted the men calling him by his former title—"A Captain needs must by definition own a ship," as they well knew—but eventually he had relented. Truth be told, he still thought of the Duffle as his. *God willing, she'll be mine again.*

"It's her, right enough," he said, reaching out for the spyglass. He trained it in on the bay, looking for where he knew she must be. Movement—shadows within shadows—confirmed it. "A fresh coat of pitch, but that's her. Go alert the militia chief and tell him to send out a team to hold the dock once their teams are ashore."

"Aye, sir," the young man replied, rushing off to obey. Another solider came in as soon as the lad had left.

"Captain Robert, orders?" It was Mitchell, who he'd been training with in a more covert style of armed combat.

"Get your team, Lieutenant Mitchell, and meet me west of the docks, station *red*." Robert smiled. "We have a ship to take."

His smile was met by a snap salute. "Aye, sir," Mitchell responded, "Right away."

Robert pulled on a tactical vest; something he'd been working on with Daniels, which involved keeping everything he might need for defensive purposes in a secure rigging he could get to easily. He also pulled a dark cloth mask over his face, as well as dark gloves so that his skin wouldn't stand out against the rest of the shadows. Then he ran quietly down to the docks and took up his position in time to see the Monkey's Duffle slip silently up to the docks.

Mitchell and his team pulled up a moment later and they huddled in the shadowed alcove of what they had labeled station red. Several locations of defensive positioning had been indicated across the surrounding locale of the town, from the base of the forest up the hill and around to the water's edge in both directions. It allowed them to allocate soldiers to a precise and defensible position quickly and efficiently.

"Send your first team in, have them wait for our signal," he told Mitchell. The lieutenant turned to three of his men and pointed towards the ship. They nodded and headed down to the closest point of the docks and lowered themselves down into the water.

As another part of their plan, the harbor guard had also affixed a series of oil lamps at the edge of the docks—something that had not been there the last time the pirate ship had docked here—and the pirates' shore party instantly recognized the difference. Previously, it had been possible to come straight from the far end of the dock all the way into the town before one needed risk a chance of being seen.

Now, however, the flickering lamps cast a brilliance across the entire area. To get close enough to douse it would bring them out of the obscuring embrace of the night; trying to knock the lamp down would pose the risk of crashing an oil fire onto the wooden dock.

From their vantage point, Robert and company could see a few of the pirates now huddled together as they debated how to respond. Robert held up his hand to keep his people steady.

After a minute or two, one of the pirates hurried forward and awkwardly climbed the pole to try and douse the lamp. A moment later, he climbed back down and ran back to the rest of the pirates. Another few moments of discussion, and the entire band ran through the spheres of light from the two lamps and moved quickly into the town.

Mitchell tapped Robert on the shoulder, gesturing meaningfully towards the docks, but Robert shook his head. He knew they'd figure out a way to deal with the lamps; the point was to keep them night-blind as long as possible as they made their way into the town. It also bought them a few extra minutes for their other men to get into position.

The next step in their preparations had been to paint all the dock-facing buildings stark white. This allowed them to easily count the men who rushed into the town from the pirate ship. Robert counted silently, keeping track of the number of pirates, and calculating how many that should leave on the ship. It had been almost two months since they'd last been here, Robert figured, and they'd had a full crew back then. Unless they'd encountered trouble, it was unlikely that Captain Gadrick (the thought of the name alone forced Robert to swallow against the rising bile the other man conjured up) would have taken on new crew.

Another minute, and the pirates had all gone ashore; at least, all who would be going. Robert held up four fingers, indicating a rough count of how many dozen men had gone past. Mitchell, who had also been counting nodded to confirm the number. Robert grimaced; *that was more pirates ashore than the militia would be expecting. On the other hand, that means less men to defend the ship.*

Robert lowered his hand, pointing once more ahead and towards the ship. They moved from their place of concealment and swiftly moved towards the docks. His men wore soft-soled shoes, sewn together from cured deerskin. Robert had been teaching them all to walk like the people out in *the Tribe*, quiet like the wind. They were fairly good, most of them. Two of the men—who were solid combatants but never did manage to master walking quietly, Robert and Mitchell waved on into the front of the line. These two, unlike the rest, wore regular leather soled boots and carried a pair of nearly empty barrels in their hands.

Robert knew Tyler Tats or someone similar would be waiting by with a team of defenders to prevent boarding. Their orders had always been; "unless you hear gunfire, the first person not carrying goods onto the ship gets a shot in the gullet."

Two pirates waited on the docks by the hull of the ship, where the casting lines kept the ship tied off. Their attention was fixed on the two men carrying the barrels—so much so that Robert and Mitchell were able to silence them and carefully lay their unconscious bodies on the dock without making a sound.

If Tyler Tats was still manning the defensive position, that would leave a dozen men on the deck, a dozen more in the rigging in preparation for a quick departure, with a final dozen below decks to man the cannons. The first two were absolutely essential to keep the ship safe, the third was just to encourage the harbor cannons to stop firing at them as they fled.

But if his count was right, there were only a couple dozen pirates left on the ship, period. By chance, one of the cannon ports had been left open near them. Robert risked a look inside and saw…no one. He tapped Mitchell on the shoulder and pointed inside.

Mitchell tapped two of his smaller men and gestured into the porthole. They squirmed dexterously into the ship's interior and quickly scouted the interior as they moved into position at the bottom of the stairs.

Robert gestured to the two barrel-carrying decoy men, and they quickly strode up the gangplank and onto the ship. The Captain and the Lieutenant waited below with the rest of their men in the shadows beside the hull.

Above deck, they could hear the two men with the barrels being addressed by Tyler, and Robert breathed a sigh of relief. He knew well how Tyler worked—for their plan to be successful, they needed as few surprises as possible.

The men dropped the barrels at the same time onto the main deck; loud enough to send a vibration through the ship. That had been their pre-arranged signal for Mitchell's first team to move in; had there been any trouble, they would have set the barrels down, one at a time.

Robert put his right foot up on the bottom of the plank and was about to walk up when one of their two "barrel men" reappeared at the rail.

"Come on up, sirs, you have to see this."

A moment later, Robert was jumping down to the deck and pulled his mask off in amazement. The only pirate on deck was Tyler Tats himself, hands in the air.

"Captain *Robert*!?" he exclaimed, clearly confused. "But—but - my god, I thought you were dead!"

"Respawned," Robert said offhandedly, even though the word made as much sense to him as it did to the others. "Rather, Gadrick's as bad at shooting as the doc was good at healing. But what happened? Where is everyone?"

Tyler shook his head; Robert could see now a fresh scar across the man's cheek that hadn't been there before. "No-Nails tried to commandeer the ship when he came back without you—we were bein' gone at by the towers something awful, so most of us just let it ride til we got clear. But out on the water, we set to talking and something in his story didn't hold up, so we told him to get stuffed. Somma his men, though, fought and we lost a lot of the crew. We threw him and his die-hards off the ship and sailed around for a bit til we started running low on stock." Tyler shrugged. "We didn't know where else to go, so we came back here."

The three men they'd sent over the water dropped down off the far rail, and the men who'd snuck into the belowdecks all burst up onto the deck at that moment, startling Tyler into a moment of stunned silence.

His expression changed to an impressed smile. "You woulda had us, sure enough, even if I'd had a crew along," he conceded.

Robert chuckled. "So why'd you send all the men into town, then? You should've known it left the ship vulnerable."

At that moment, two shots rang out at the far edge of town, followed by a pause and a third shot.

"That's the all clear," Mitchell nodded to Robert. "The militia was faster than I expected."

"You don't understand," Tyler corrected. "We didn't come here to steal."

Robert and his lieutenant exchanged a pair of confused glances.

"We came back to *surrender*."

Sure enough, the militia leaders reported in a few minutes later to confirm that the pirates had gone ashore and gathered in the town square, milling about in plain sight with their guns and swords on the ground in front of them.

The pirates were painfully undernourished, and several of them were actually quite ill and dehydrated. To a man, they swore to leave behind the life of violent piracy and offered to assist the town in whatever way they could.

Robert had the clever idea of utilizing them as a naval defense for the various trade ships that came and went from the Nikada bay, a decision which over the years to come would prove financially advantageous for the town.

Soon after, Robert was given a position of authority within the town and moved into a beautiful home with a bedroom view that overlooked the town and the bay, all the way past the Shadow's Fangs and into the blue horizon.

It all seemed…too good to be true.

The dreams had stopped coming to him while he slept. Robert woke lightly as the sunlight crept in through wind-stirred curtains and Miriam stretched beside him, the nearness and warmth of her skin sending a contented thrill across his body. *This*, he thought, *is a good morning*.

He kissed her lightly on the cheek as he slipped from her embrace and left their bed, crossing to first throw a thin robe around his shoulders before walking towards the balcony of their apartment. His gaze fell on a desk by the doors, upon which sat a strange pair of goggles. His hand reached out, as if out of habit, and picked them up so he could look at them.

Strange thing. Why do I keep it, he wondered?

He looked through the lenses, and immediately yanked the goggles away, wincing in discomfort. *Really distorted, these things; they don't even work.* He set them back on the desk, making himself a mental note to throw them out later as he parted the curtains and stepped out onto the balcony.

The sunlight was descending down past the tall cone of the always-smoldering mountain that rose to the east of the town and creating countless glimmers upon the tips of the waves in the bay. Only a few clouds dotted the sky, tall billowing puffs that looked as if they were made of cotton. It was indeed a good morning, Robert thought to himself. He combed his fingers through the short hair of his head; *this feels so much better than that tangled mess I'd worn before. Why had I let it grow out so much in the first place,* he wondered?

His eyebrows furrowed together. There had been a reason, hadn't there? It had once seemed so important, like it meant something, but he couldn't quite put his finger on it.

Like a strange itch he couldn't quite scratch, he tried to think back over the years he'd grown it out. Years? Had it been years? It seemed like he'd been in the town for years, but that couldn't be correct, could it?

He began thinking back in his mind over the events that had happened since his arrival in town, working backwards.

He and Miriam had been married… *had that been just yesterday? Last week? Last month? A year ago?* It was hard to remember, now. How had they met? Oh yes, he'd been shot.

Robert blinked, surprised. He pulled his robe open just enough to look at his chest, and saw no scar, no wound, no indication of a wound. *Was I shot? But, I remember it… don't I?*

And who shot me? Why did they shoot me? That doesn't make...sense, does it? People don't just go around shooting people, do they?

His eyes rested on a ship with black sails that stood moored to the far dock of the harbor. *The Monkey's Duffel, that's right, isn't it? Was that my ship? Is that why they call me Captain?*

A stream of memories began to pour out and through his mind, and a hint of dreams already forgotten stood beside them. *What does it mean? Who was that? Was that me? Where was I, and how did I get...?*

"Here you are, lover," Miriam said, sliding up behind him and reaching her arms to embrace him from behind. "The bed's too cold without you."

Instinctively, he turned his back to the docks and his lips sought out his wife's perfect mouth. They kissed; he breathed once more, taking in the scent of her and exhilarated in the rush of sensations her touch brought to his skin.

She led him back through the curtains, away from the balcony, back to their bed. Thoughts of dreams or pirate ships or absent gunshot wounds vanished in the intoxication of her touch, her kiss, her breath and her soft moans of delight.

This was the memory that mattered, Robert decided.

The other memories—whatever they were and wherever they came from—were pale and lifeless against the reality of this world.

A faint crackle and hiss faded in the back of his mind; something called a *video game* at last powered off, as Miriam's kiss enveloped him, and vanished into the ether to which all discarded thoughts go.

<shut down console? Yes/No>

<Yes>

BOOKS BY REN CUMMINS

Tales of the Dead Man:
Steel & Sky (book 1)
Sun & Stone (book 2)

https://www.renwritings.com/
https://www.doceblant.com/ren-cummins/

Treasure

by T. L. Vale

Emma lifted her head to survey the open blueness of the sky and water. The air held the salt scrubbed freshness of the sea. Wind gusted through her hair, stinging her cheeks as loose tendrils whipped her face.

Ducking her head, she glimpsed a small irregular shape poking out from the smooth sand. Picking it up, Emma lurched, gasping. For the instant before she dropped the rusty metal piece, she had been somewhere else, crowded by smelly men, in a dim lit wooden room. They were looking, at a drawing on a thin scrap of leather which lay unrolled across a table and held flat by an old wood handled pistol and pewter tankard.

"Emma!" Auntie raced over and steadied her. "What is it? Did you cut your hand?"

"No," She pointed to the crusty little metal square, that lay on the sand. "I…I had a kind-a-of daydream."

"Ah!" Auntie bent and scooped up the old metal scrap. Holding it between her hands, she closed her eyes and visibly relaxed. "It's an old brass buckle!"

Her cousins ran over. "What is it mom?" Can we see?"

Auntie stood for a moment and kept her hands around the object. "Let's do some psychometry," she said to everyone. "Everything vibrates, and if we just listen, we can sometimes sense things about an object. The way that you do this, is you cup the object in your hands, close your eyes, clear your mind, and relax, Then, just allow yourself to experience. Sometimes, you'll see pictures, sometimes you'll feel as if you are somewhere else," Auntie winked at Emma. "Other times you'll get ideas, you may hear sounds or smells or even tastes. Psychometry is an ancient art of reading the energy of an item by which you can tell things about who has owned it and where it has been.

She handed the piece to Alicia who stood quietly for a moment, then she smiled. "I see a pirate ship." Everyone giggled.

"You've got pirates on your brain." said Henry as he reached to take the object from her.

He stood for a moment grimacing and then shook his head. I hear seagulls, I smell seawater, it's cold, it's dark. I feel like I'm in a wooden box. It makes me seasick!" He thrust the object at Abigail.

Little Abigail pushed it into the center of her forehead, between her eyebrows. "It belongs to a big man, he was really, really mean and he hurt people. I don't like him."

Abigail extended her hand. Emma looked at that crusty metal square and their faces, it was obvious that they wanted her to play too. She picked it up and cupped it as Auntie had shown them. Emma slowed her breath, softened her shoulders and instantly she was back in the crowded room with the smell of sweaty bodies and foul-smelling air, she thought it might be kerosene. She felt suffocated and panicked. Men were talking in low whispers about the map; they were speaking Spanish, but she didn't understand.

"I hear words in Spanish," she said shaking her head. I think they are talking to him about looking for something, it sounds like 'Gasparilla.' Yes, that's what they call the mean looking man.

Emma offered the buckle to her aunt, "No, it's yours, you found it, keep it. I would encourage you to write down what you experienced. The more you practice psychometry the better you'll get. I'll take a look on the Internet when we get home and see if we can find a captain sarsaparilla."

Everybody laughed, "Not sarsaparilla, Mama. "Gas, he's got gas," everyone tittered.

"Whatever," said Auntie turning to walk lazily back to the car.

Later that afternoon Alicia squealed as she looked at something on her laptop, "Here he is! Jose Gaspar, they called him Gasparilla. He's a pirate! You found something that belong to a real pirate! This is so cool!"

"That's him, that's the man I saw!" Emma gasped. "I saw him. They were all crowded around the table in that small wooden room, it was rocking, like maybe it was in the water. It was so cold. Something was in the air that made my lungs hurt, I had trouble breathing, I wanted to cough and my eyes watered. The light was so dim and dusty."

"I bet it was a treasure map!" Henry leaned over his sister's shoulder to read. "Do it again and look to see where the treasure is marked on the map!"

Sitting down Emma placed the little scrap of metal in her hand and begin to do what Henry had told her. This time, there were men shouting and pushing. Emma felt as if she was in a crowd, pushed up against a tall wooden fence. "Everyone is shoving and yelling. I don't think I want to do this."

Henry touched her shoulder and insisted she relax, "Now turn and look around," he coached. "What do you see?"

"Lots of angry men trying to push open a gate in a big fence like at a fort. There's so much anger and shouting and yelling."

"Okay," Henry was talking very quietly, "take a big breath and when you release it, push yourself to the other side of the fence.

Suddenly, she was on the other side of the fence, "Oh, my God!" Emma's eyes flew open. "They hung him!"

"Yeah!" Henry smacked his side, then popped his fist. Everyone turned to scowl at him.

"How am I doing this?" Emma's eyes locked on her aunt's.

"Everything in life vibrates and for some reason those vibrations can imprint on objects. I think it's an emotional thing, the more intense the feelings the stronger the impression on the item. Photographs, rings, precious items, often have these energies on them. If we are sensitive, we can touch in and experience what happened to cause the imprint. Our brain does not know the difference of whether it is now or in the past."

"Will you try again?" Abigail asked, "I want to know if you can see the map so that we can find the treasure."

Auntie pulled Emma in for a hug. "First of all, I'd like you to write down everything from the very beginning." she handed Emma a lovely journal book. "Keep your notes in this."

Emma toyed with the corroded brass buckle as she wrote her memories from the psychometry experiences. As she described the map, she realized that she could remember several landmarks and sketched them out, showing them to her auntie.

"Great! Let's pull up Google Earth and see if we can find these landmarks." Her aunt said sitting down to the computer.

"Look!" Alicia pushed forward and twisted the journal "Turn the map this way. See? It's Charlotte's Harbor!"

"Yes, but there's a lot of land there and I don't see any way to know exactly where the treasure is buried. But we can drive down there tomorrow and take a look around."

Early the next morning the family drove up and down the coastline of Charlotte Harbor exploring all the tourist history sites. Standing next to a Banyan tree on the Edison-Ford Estates, Emma fingered a deeply carved X on the tree as she held the little metal buckle. "I feel like I've been here before," she said, turning to walk along the river. "There's a museum over here, can we go in?"

Auntie nodded and followed her in.

"Look!" Henry grabbed Emma by the hand and pulled her to the back room of the museum On the far wall, mounted in a glass case, hung the tattered remains of an old leather map. On closer inspection, Emma knew it was the map she had seen in her vision. Under the display hung a plaque which read, "Treasure Map allegedly marking the location of The Pirate Gasparilla's Treasure. A small clear plastic label was pasted on the glass to the left of the large faded black X. It read, "The Charlotte County Historical Center was relocated to this site on July 27, 2018."

Henry threw up his hands, "What good is a treasure map that only leads to the map and not the treasure?"

Everyone laughed, but as Emma laid her hand on the glass covering the old map, she saw a metal banded trunk with leather straps. It sat beneath a large Banyan tree as a pirate dug a hole among the roots. in which to hide his treasure.

BOOKS BY TERESA CAROL

All Spooked Up
How to Spook Yourself Up

https://www.teresacarol.com/
https://www.doceblant.com/authors/paranormal-investigator-and-intuitive-author-teresa-arol/

The Entity

BY A. M. CRANE

"Wilkins!"

Melissa's voice sounded hollow against the cavernous hallway stretched ahead of her. It ran alongside the main building. Forgotten artwork dotted the stone walls, placed there centuries earlier. No one remembered the painted portraits or landscapes that hung there. No one cared.

"Wilkins, where are you?" She called out again, but the only answer was the faint echo of footsteps that scuttled ahead of her. Unsure whether her own footfall, or that of creatures living in the darkness made the sound, she hesitated, hoping the resonance would fade away. It did not.

She flashed the light from her cell phone to the wall and caught a shadow scurry out of the beam. Its tail flicked to one side just before the vermin looked at her with glowing eyes and darted out of sight.

"Rats. Literally. What am I doing here?" Melissa turned the light to the opposite side of the hallway and saw another rodent run across the face of a regal lady memorialized in oil and framed in gilded wood. "Shame."

She took another step, forcing her eyes to stay focused on the floor ahead of her. *Step on one of those and it's over!* The thought passed and she stepped again, this time with a little more determination. *Wilkins owes me for this. It'll cost him extra for the next artifact I bring to him.* She huffed and shouted, "Wilkins!"

It came first as a breeze, something brushed lightly along her arm, raising the hairs of her neck as it passed. She flashed the cell phone's light toward it then behind her. Nothing. Again, the wisp of air rushing by raised the flesh of her arms and she felt herself begin to tremble.

"Who's there?"

A course whisper sounded in the echo. Not her voice this time—it was deep and breathy—an otherworldly rasp.

Leave this place.

"Wilkins? Is that you?" Melissa's plea mimicked the tremble she felt rush her body. "I demand to know who's there!"

Leave…a'fore it's too late.

Ahead, in the distance, a shadow moved. She lifted her phone toward it but the light from her screen flickered, and then died. "Damn!" Melissa shook the phone but there was no response. With no phone and no light, she was alone in the museum's forgotten passageway with the rodents… and the shadow.

Ye've no business here, lass. Be gone, says I.

"You're not Wilkins."

Raspy laughter hissed and Melissa was unsure whether it was a wayward gust of wind from some unknown fracture in the building or the specter she sensed toyed with her. She felt the eyes of the portraits stare at her.

"What do you want?"

Aye, then…and what seek ye, missy?

The shadow moved closer. Melissa froze, unable to run, afraid to step on unseen creatures. Her limbs wouldn't obey her, anyway. She knew the entity smelled her fear. It moved again.

"I…I seek Wilkins." Melissa wished she could retract the comment as soon as she spoke. "I mean, I'm here to meet Wilkins. He owns this place. You shouldn't be here without him knowing—"

I've sommat for ye.

She felt a hand grasp at her arm and jumped back. "Don't touch me!"

Again, the raspy laughter echoed and she stepped back. "I need to find Wilkins." She turned, ready to trace her steps back to the main entrance, but the shadow moved in front of her. "Please. Let me go."

Nay. Ye've ventured this far an' I've sommat for ye.

"I don't want anything. I just want to go. Please."

The hand pushed her backward and she felt her heart race. Would this be the place she would die—alone, in a forgotten hallway with only the dusty paintings as witnesses? The rats would notice. They would creep forward slowly and begin to feast. No one would miss her, not even that good-looking guy who'd been in the library a few hours earlier. Patrick—he seemed nice enough, but the Sullivan House had captured him by now, she was sure of it. He'd never be seen again either. Melissa shook the thought away and stared at the shadow.

"Don't kill me…not here…please. Do your dark deed elsewhere, someplace they'll find me, so the rats won't eat me. Please?" Her voice sounded weak.

Laughter wheezed as the shadow circled her. She felt the hand brush her cheek. Then, suddenly, it gripped her back. She flinched and closed her eyes, waiting for the sting of a knife to open her throat. Perhaps the crack of her neck would echo next as the entity broke her bones. "Do it!" she screamed.

Only laughter, whispering the length of the corridor.

I've no need of another body, lass, crowded as these quarters be. Nay, I've sommat for ye.

Melissa opened her eyes and startled. The entity's gaze pierced the darkness; its yellow eyes staring only inches from hers. The smell of decay and rotted teeth made her gag. Dank, salty air suddenly filled her lungs and she felt the floor begin to sway.

"Who are you?" she whispered, barely able to breathe, fighting back a sudden feeling of overwhelming seasickness.

Capt'n, they call me. Black be me moniker. Foul deeds follow an eternity waiting here until I enter the house.

"Sullivan House?"

Aye.

"You're waiting to enter the Sullivan House? Why?" It was a ridiculous question and Melissa knew it. Only the dead, who had yet to pay for their dark deeds in life, went to the Sullivan House. This ghost was evil and waited its turn.

Retribution must be paid.

"I understand. It will be difficult for you there." Melissa tried to feign sympathy in hopes the entity would let her go.

Do not feel pity for me, missy.

"No…no, I don't. I only wish to leave and find Wilkins. I have business with him."

Indeed, ye do—as do I.

Melissa swallowed. The hand moved from her back, along her side, hesitating before resting on her belly. "Please…" she whispered.

You're not with child, though you should be. 'Tis better this way.

She felt a rush pass through her, nearly toppling her over. Bile rose to the back of her throat and she thought she would vomit as she fell to her knees. "Please, have mercy…"

No mercy for those holdin' to their secrets.

Melissa wretched. Gasping, she clawed at the entity, grasping only icy emptiness. Its yellow eyes glowed and she heard its laugh at her again. As she glanced up, she saw the markings of what looked like a curved sword tucked within a sash. Again, the scent of seawater sickened her as the entity passed through her once more.

"Stop…please," she whispered.

The dead suffer more than the living. Those who wait for retribution be taunted with desires an' passions an' hunger from the livin'.

"I am not your toy."

Laughter pierced the walls, ricocheting against the hollow, scattering the rodents. *I do not seek desires o' the flesh, missy—least of all ye, little mouse —though in my day I was indeed hearty. Nay, I hunger for freedom, the sea, and its bounty.*

"You…you sailed the seas?" Another question she wished she hadn't asked. Quickly, changing the subject, she cleared her throat and stood. "What is it then you'd have of me, sir?"

I've sommat for ye.

The brush of a hand traced her leg, dropping something at her feet. She glanced at the object but did not pick it up. "What is that?"

Treasure. Take it…but bring the token to me, else return to take your soul, I will. The House cannot contain me forever and I'll hunt ye down, Melissa.

She gasped. "You know my name?"

Indeed, I do. I know more than that, missy. A shadowy hand waved over the object at her feet. *Use it. Find the treasure and bring me the token. Ye'll know it when we see it. Do not fail or the dead be your companions, says I.*

Melissa bent over and picked up an ancient, brass sextant. Turning it over, she studied the marks etched along its sides. She guessed it must have been nearly 400 years old.

"And what do I call you, when I seek you out, spirit?" She glanced up and saw nothing but darkness. The entity had disappeared though she sensed him near. "Huh? What do I call you?"

From deep within the darkness, she heard the whisper of the wind. A rush of salty mist blew in the distance and the echo answered her:

Pirate.

BOOKS BY A. M. CRANE

Sullivan House

https://www.doceblant.com/authors/a-m-crane-sullivan/

A Hatchling's Time to Fly

By Ren Cummins

There were plenty of challenges with being the daughter to your people's spiritual advisor, but right near the top of the list was not being able to win arguments. Not a single one of them, Sjora thought. She sat in the back of the assembly hall, watching as a dozen citizens of the floating citadel Jaaris B'kaan waited in their queue to address the Song Mistress. While she watched and waited, Sjora looked at each of the supplicants in turn, trying to imagine what wishes blossomed in their hearts.

Sick child, weather inquiry, cracks in their kitchen wall, changes in their work schedule, interpretation of the old tomes on flea prevention… she almost chuckled at the perceived silliness of it all. How her mother was able to listen to their various crises and not just throw something hard at them for not figuring it out on their own was a hidden talent Sjora could only hope one day to acquire. When the next person stood and announced they were concerned by a potential mis-translation of ancient creature care involving parasites, Sjora could contain her amusement no longer and laughed aloud.

She felt her mother's gaze on her before she looked up and confirmed it. The Song Mistress made a simple gesture indicating Sjora join her beside her chair and, with the eyes of the room upon her, she had little choice but to submit.

Slowly, she walked to her mother's side and did her best to appear the humble and obedient daughter.

Initially, she kept her eyes straight forward as her mother had instructed her; not lingering too long upon another's face lest it cause them discomfort, accompanying the casual glance with an undefined softness that reassured the other party freedom from condemnation. "There are no evil requests in the Tower of Harmony," it was said. Sjora thought that while there may not be evil requests, there could still be an awful lot of stupid ones.

As if her mother could sense her thoughts, the Song Mistress leaned slightly in Sjora's direction and whispered deftly without a single movement of her lips: "Please set aside your rebellious soul for a few moments, little one, and listen."

To her part, Sjora was able to resist making a loud sigh or rolling her eyes in defiant frustration. She simply nodded her head and retained the same expressionless look on her face. Her mother had been emphasizing the need for her to learn more about the responsibilities she would one day bear when she became the Song Mistress, herself. That seemed like a lifetime away, Sjora reasoned, and her mother hadn't taken the title until she was almost three times Sjora's age. There would plenty of time for her to learn what she needed to learn. For now, Sjora just wanted to feel the wind on her face, play with her friend Parris and, when she had to practice fighting, beat up the insufferably annoying Tarik.

Her mother placed one hand on her shoulder, applying the slightest pressure on her collarbone. Sjora realized that her mind had been wandering again, just enough to bring attention to herself. The room had fallen silent and once again everyone was staring at her. She wasn't even sure what she'd done until her mother adjusted her posture for her. She'd been slouching. Slouching! She bit her tongue at the thought of having committed one of the unforgivable sins. Gods forfend that she, twelve seasons of age, be mindlessly bored to tears by hearing people complain about rats. Or was it lice? Ticks? She hadn't been paying attention; she didn't know. She didn't care.

After the Song Mistress gestured for him to continue, the man resumed his commentary on how he felt the proper solution for skin irritation ought to be managed, when another man standing a few paces back in line leaped forward to interrupt him. The two men began fighting with each other—they were apparently on different sides of the flea prevention debate—and Sjora decided that this would be as good a time as any to make her escape. Passing quickly behind her mother's chair, she ran along the inner curve of the wall towards a pair of curtains that concealed a side exit never used by the main body of the Sky People's citizenry. Sneaking past the sword masters at the main entrance, she slipped over the railing of the slight incline that led into the Tower of Harmony and dropped into one of the gardens below. The shrubs and vines provided ample natural cover for the girl as she sped away from the tower towards the stables.

The stables greeted her with the familiar scents of hay and other feed cultivated from the vertical gardens found on the south-facing slopes of the citadel. Protected from the harsh winds they faced while the citadel moved from one resting point to another, the crops were only part of the tribe's resolution to live harmoniously with the land. Another prominent feature was in how they lived symbiotically with the creatures of Aerthos.

She had asked the stablemasters to stop curtseying and bowing as she entered. It was supposed to make her feel special, she figured, but it had the reverse effect. It made her feel like she didn't belong here among the caretakers. At least among the animals, she felt like they were on the same level: just beings struggling for survival, without other social cares or responsibilities. She did her best to both respond to and ignore the various good morning pleasantries, scratching the heads of a few of the creatures on her way back to the larger flying beasts, coming to halt at one in particular, her eyes widening at its relative emptiness.

"Parris?" she inquired, realizing that as the animal was not here, her question was more for the caretakers than the animal itself.

One of the caretakers passed her, pushing a tall wheelbarrow full of grain. "Sorry, miss Sjora—Parris hasn't been back since last night."

"But she's always back by sunrise!"

The young man nodded, but continued on about his work, apparently unconcerned about the creature's absence. Sjora growled, doubling up her fists in anger as she sought out the stablemaster.

She eventually found the woman in one of the smaller pens, caring for a pair of recent newborn vantrells. The whole citadel had been honored to have the pair hatch here—a feat normally only seen in the wild, and never as a pair of twin hatchlings. The vantrells were a traditionally secretive breed of fliers, generally nesting only in a secluded series of caves near the eastern cliffs of the continent. The mother had been discovered in one of the uninhabited storage areas near the base of the citadel and led up into the stables when they learned it was also tending to a damaged wing. The caretakers had braced and healed its wing and perhaps in response, the vantrell mother had remained here until the eggs had hatched. In spite of its genetic predispositions, it allowed the Sky People to tend to its young as well, returning several times a day to check on its young while it roamed further and further on its healed wings.

"Yes, Miss Sjora," the woman asked, not even turning to regard her. Sjora couldn't quite decide if she approved of the difference in her disposition when compared with the rest of the workers or if it just annoyed her more. "I take it from your exclamations that there is a problem?"

"Parris," Sjora said. "She hasn't come back from her hunting last night. I think something's wrong."

"That is possible," the woman replied, setting one of the infant vantrells down while the other climbed up into her lap. "The koravin are migratory, as you know. She may have decided it is time to move on and be with a different herd."

"She wouldn't do that!" Sjora insisted. "She loves it here. And…" The words couldn't quite come to her lips; couldn't quite get past the stiffening in her throat.

The stablemaster plucked the second vantrell from her lap and stood up, carefully walking towards the fencing that kept the small animals from wandering away. "And what, miss?"

"And she was my friend!" Sjora blurted out. She instantly felt embarrassed by the statement. She knew the law, she knew the creatures. The animals did not belong to the Sky People any more than the Sky People belonged to them. It was a partnership and an alliance, but casual in nature with the creatures free to leave of their own will, provided it was safe for them to do so.

"That may be true," the older woman said softly, "but who is to say where one must fly? When one hears the song, they must follow the melody."

Sjora fought back the threat of tears behind her eyes, holding up the crystal she wore around her neck. "But she always comes back to be with me," she said with trembling lips. "She can't be gone; I've known her forever."

Seeing the young girl at the verge of tears, the stablemaster reached out and held Sjora to her breast. "It is all well," she whispered. "I am sure she is well, and you will see her again."

"She can still find me, wherever she goes, right? Because I bound our crystals together so she will always know where I am, no matter where the citadel flies?"

The older woman nodded, patting Sjora's head. "The crystals are bound forever, miss. She will always know where you are and will always be able to come back to you."

Sjora could hear unspoken words in the woman's sentence. "If she can."

The woman did not respond, but after a moment made a gesture of smoothing out Sjora's dark braided hair. "I believe these gentlemen are looking for you."

The girl turned to see two of the sword masters standing in the doorway, looking back at her.

"Tell my mother I will talk to her later," she growled.

They both looked uncomfortably at one another. "We, um… miss, she asked us to bring you to her straight away."

"You should go," the stablemaster said softly. "I shall send word when Parris returns."

Clearly in opposition to her mandate, Sjora sighed, and began walking towards them. Only a few paces away, she opened her mouth to draw in a fair quantity of air and was satisfied to see them both take a half step back. But to their relief, she simply turned and thanked the stablemaster before turning back to them and gesturing for them to lead her to her mother.

The tower was just clearing out as they arrived. Sjora caught a few poorly-concealed expressions of frustration on some faces; she figured her mother must have cancelled the gathering as soon as she had become aware of Sjora's absence. She felt a little guilty about that but did her best to push it out of her mind. Yes, some of their concerns were valid and needed guidance, but so often she just wanted to grab them and shake them until they learned to think for themselves.

She stood at the back of the assembly area until the room was cleared out of everyone but the two men who had escorted her here, herself, and her mother. The song mistress gestured to the warriors, who bowed and left, closing the large doors behind them.

The wind whistled through the room, ruffling a pair of long tapestries against the walls. The sun was at its height in the sky above them, and sent prismatic illuminations cascading down through the stained-glass patterns set at even intervals into the walls and ceiling. It made Sjora think back on an evening she had snuck in to sit in her mother's chair during a lightning storm and danced in mad circles until she was too dizzy to stand. She recalled laying on the floor, barely able to contain the laughter.

She didn't much feel like laughing now, however.

"You may begin your apologies whenever you wish, child."

Sjora's mouth hung open. She might have been, on a better day or in a better mood, willing to at least bite her cheek and offer up a passable apology of some sort; but somehow the notion of being told to do so pushed the idea fully out of her mind. She felt her fingers curl into fists again as a pounding began to drum inside her ears.

"For what?" she heard herself say. She hadn't thought her voice had come out so loudly, but the circular acoustics in the room must have surely distorted the sound as it came back to her ears. "For leaving?"

The song mistress remained calm and slowly nodded her head.

"You didn't need me here, mother," Sjora replied, even more loudly than before. "I didn't want to be here, so I left. Or am I a prisoner here?"

Her mother's eyebrows rose sharply. "No, little one, you are not a prisoner."

"But I can't leave."

"Not when you are responsible for staying, no."

"Well, I'm glad I went, anyway," the girl said, full of righteous indignation.

"Why is that?"

"Parris is gone."

"Gone?"

"Yes. She didn't come back last night."

"Sjora…." The song mistress shook her head. "Please speak as you have been taught."

The girl took a deep breath and tried but failed to unclench her fists. "*She did not come back last night.*"

With a satisfied nod, the song mistress attended to the root of the presented problem. "Have you brought this to the attention of the stablemasters?"

"Yes, but…"

"But what?"

"They said that maybe she just decided to fly away and not come back."

"And what do you think?"

"I…don't—I do not know," she answered, correcting her speech before her mother could say anything about it.

"You do not believe them?"

"I…no, mother. I do not."

The song mistress remained silent for several moments, finally responding with a nod of her head. "Very well, then.

Let us play a game. Imagine you are the song mistress, and a young woman brings this issue to your attention. How would you respond?"

Sjora hated this game, and she would not have been the least shocked to learn her mother was aware of that fact. She was already prepared for this favored game of her mother's, however. "I would send out a team of trackers to go and find her."

"So you think she is lost?"

"No, she has a crystal on her collar that's attuned to the Compass. She always knows where we are."

"So you believe she is unable to return?"

"Maybe…I think? Perhaps."

The song mistress held on to the silence for several more moments. Sjora realized that it was not her mother who was thinking so much, as her mother was giving her time to think as well.

"This is our contract we make with the creatures of the wild, Sjora. They are free to come and go as they please, with the promise that we will never subject them to our citadel or our lives. One of every ten of them leave each handful of days, never to return, and their number is almost instantly replaced by another. It is a great balance and we are only a part of it, not its hand of destiny. And so we cannot force another to comply with our will nor restrain them to our path. I am sorry, little one, but perhaps it is simply time for you to let your friend go."

"So we aren't even going to look for her? What if she's hurt? What if she's dying out there, alone, and we never help her?"

"It is the way, little one. We must follow the path of the world. It is why our citadels float along the ley lines of Aerthos, pausing only when the energies of the world bring us to a halt. When the path ends, there we rest."

Sjora could not bear to hear another page or sentence of their philosophy at the moment. The thought of losing her closest friend was too strong, too overwhelming. She turned and moved quickly towards the entryway doors.

"Sjora, where do you think you are going?"

Sjora spun briefly to dangle the crystal she wore at her own throat. "Does it even matter? You'll just find me no matter where I go!"

She pushed open the doors with a low, almost feral growl, slipping past the guards and running home. She had been right, of course. It didn't matter where she went, her mother would always know exactly where she was.

In her room, however, she wasted no time. She threw an old pack on her bed and tossed an assortment of items onto the bed beside it. A few pair of clothes, some of her travel gear and camping supplies, as well as some traveling clothes which included rock climbing gloves and durable boots. She packed what she needed, and changed into clothes more suited to traveling in. She grabbed a brass sextant off her desk, a gift from her old teacher Johen; when she'd learned about the Compass and how ships moved differently than the citadel. She folded it down into its carrying case and slid this into a small pouch on her pack. She nearly ran down the stairs to the kitchen. She scurried between the busy cooks, grabbing some bread, cheese and dried meats, and filled a wineskin with fresh water, tucking these all into her pack and being on her way before anyone could ask questions.

The port was only a ten-minute walk from their house, and Sjora made it in five. Three ships were parked on the platforms today; she ran over to the harbormaster, a young man about twice her age named K'vald. He had always been nice to her. He had a young daughter, Sjora had sat for on a pair of occasions. He'd shown her a lot about ships that went beyond what she'd been able to learn on her own. He sized her up in the time it took her to walk over to him near his command shed.

"No flights out for you today, Sjora of the blue skies," he smiled. "The Pathmaster and the Sentinel aren't shoving off until the morning, and the Hundred Hawks is down for repairs. I can show you around them, but there's nothing to fly out on." He clapped his hands off on his tunic and tugged briefly on the straps of her pack. "Also, your mother already threatened me with a demotion if I ever let you fly out without a full complement of your protectors. So I'm going to have to pretend you're not here and that I haven't seen you all day."

Sjora frowned. "We really need to have ships of our own," she grumbled.

"Too much of a temptation," he said. "Besides, we have a stable full of animals that can take us wherever we might want to go."

"Well, maybe I will just do that, then," she said. "I am old enough to face the wild on my own."

K'vald stepped closer so his words would not travel beyond them. "You ought to take care how bold you are, Sjora. It's not like life here in the citadels—out there, you're as like to find pirates, poachers, or worse. There are creatures out there that don't see us as allies, they see us as food. They take as they like, and don't say please."

"I could just steal one of these ships, too."

"Don't even joke about that, Sjora. It's bad enough you even know how to fly them, but to commit theft of them… I don't know if even the daughter of the song mistress could walk away from that. Look, I don't know what's got your eyes looking to the horizon, but I think it's best you just get back to your normal rebellions and not try to destroy your whole world in the process."

He placed his hand on her shoulder, but she shrugged out of it, turned and left. She felt awful for doing it, but she was just too angry to try and apologize right now. She just wanted to go find her friend and nobody else seemed to care.

Her walking turned to running and even through eyes blurred by tears she found her way to her favorite place to be alone. At the fore of the citadel were lined a series of turbines, which caught the wind and channeled the force of its gusts into energy that fueled the Compass crystal at the heart of the citadel. From time to time, engineers came up this way to check on the turbines but aside from them, Sjora knew she could come here and be by herself. She climbed one of the lookout towers, took off her pack and buried her face in her hands until the tears at last gave way to a numb peace of mind. She felt only slightly better, but no more hopeful than she had before.

Sunset came and went, and Sjora realized that she had not brought nearly enough food for her trip, regardless of how long she thought it would have taken. She decided that this would make for a good learning opportunity for the next time she would need to commandeer a ship as part of a rescue-themed adventure. She had packed up and taken the first step down when motion outside caught her attention and froze her in her tracks.

It was a person, wearing a cloak to disguise their silhouette. They were moving quietly, too, and quickly. For a moment, her mouth hung open in preparation of calling out an alarm, but if the person continued moving in their current direction, they were going to run squarely into the night watch anyway. Strangely, all she could think of was the other voice in her head that kept her wondering how the person got onto the floating citadel in the first place. Trusting that the guards would make quick work of any sort of thievery or mischief the person might be up to, Sjora decided to solve one particular mystery before doubling back to keep an eye on them.

She waited until the figure had vanished before she snuck down the rest of the way to the ground. She moved towards the edge of the citadel and stepped over the short protective wall that stood a meter from the edge. A pair of pitons had been stuck deeply into the rocky surface and supported a rope ladder leading down over the ledge.

Taking another defensive glance to ensure the unknown person hadn't turned back, Sjora knelt down and peered over to see what the ladder was connected to. A few dozen meters down, she saw one of the most beautiful things her eyes had ever seen.

It was an airship; a twin ballonet dirigible with an open canopy, two rear propellers and small enough to be piloted by one person. She had seen larger vehicles, loud filthy monstrosities powered by coal or oil that left thick grey smears across the sky. This, though, was small but elegant; floating with a small touch of power to urge its path from here to there. When she had dreamed of leaving the citadel—which was more often than she cared to admit—this was the sort of vehicle where she imagined herself at the controls. Aerthos had put her very wishes in the palms of her hands. Right here, down that ladder lay the key to her freedom.

She played out a series of quick scenarios in her mind—of cornering the crew on their way back to the ship and convincing them to take her along and search for Parris. No, she realized—if their intentions were nefarious, they certainly would be unlikely to entertain her request. Definitely not if they were discussing it here on the citadel soil. But if she was already on the ship when they returned…

Before she had fully rationalized her actions, she was already a third of the way down the slick ladder. Even forcing herself to slow down lest she slip and fall the half-kilometer or so to the ground below, she descended quickly and took a moment to examine the deck.

The controls were locked, the ship ordered to follow the speed and direction of the citadel it had been lashed to. She gave the yoke a slight pull, but the ship would not respond. Sjora then noticed a small indentation on the control panel. A keyhole.

"Locked?" she grumbled. "What kind of person leaves their ship locked?"

At the rear of the ship, just in front of the engines, stood a small structure which turned out to be a hatchway leading down into the rest of the ship. She moved quickly but quietly, still concerned about the possibility of crew-members below deck.

Her concerns of other inhabitants were brushed away in the minutes it took to explore the cabin. It consisted mostly of a cargo area, two small cabins and a common area. But the smell was the worst of it. Initially she thought it was just a toilet backed up, but when she more closely examined the common area and small kitchen, she realized just what it was the owner of this ship did for their living. Skins and bones and other animal traces were visible, laid out to dry and sorted into various components. Now it made sense—whoever this person was, they were a poacher. Hunting and killing animals just for the things they could make money on. Which was what they had come to the citadel for—their animals!

Sjora turned to run back up the stairs when something shiny caught her attention on the top of one of the small containers on the table in the common room. Without quite knowing why, she walked over to it, and saw what had caught her gaze: Parris' crystal. Sjora picked it up and turned it over in her hands to notice a dark smudge of dried blood marking one of the facets. A low humming began to fill her ears, but she gave it no heed. Instead, she walked to the cargo area and took a closer look than she had the first time, noticing the sealed crates and the occasional stain of blood here or there. Her hands trembled. Any thought she had previously entertained regarding politely asking the ship owner to ferry her here or there was gone.

On the other hand, she wasn't sure what she *would* do. She only had her practice baton, keyed to a simple musical note; by itself it wouldn't do much. Only being twelve seasons of age, she had yet to be taught any of the combat magic. However, on a pair of occasions, Johen had performed a few different war songs. She couldn't remember all the notes, but she might know enough to help her. She remembered back, trying to draw the notes out of her memory, when she heard a pair of boots drop onto the deck above. She looked for a place to hide, but only moments later she felt the ship shifting to her left, and the propellers began to churn the air away from their previous course. It was more than just a small ship, she realized—it was fast!

She paced back and forth in the small cabin, trying to decide what her options might be, but the crystal in her hand moved her towards a choice she would never before have considered. She placed the crystal in one of the pouches of her pack and pulled out her baton. She stowed the pack beneath the cot in one of the rooms, mentally promising that she'd be back for it later. Then she made her way up the stairs and quietly peered out the main hatchway.

The shadowed figure was at the controls, peering out into the darkness as they flew. His cloak was gone, but then she saw what appeared to be a pile of cloth near his feet. Her blood boiled when she realized the bundle of cloth was moving.

Extending the baton, she felt the familiar vibrations of the practice melody—a tune of protection, little more—but she added the notes of one of Johen's songs over the top of it. It was in the same key and danced as a slight harmonic to the core tone. In her anger, she did not even pause to warn the person or declare her intent to bring them back to the citadel for their crimes. She wanted the entire scenario to be over. As the melody she hummed reached its crescendo, she drew the fully extended staff over her shoulder and down across the pilot's head. A flash of lightning sparked across the staff and across the condensation of the flooring, temporarily blinding Sjora and sending her sliding back towards the rear of the airship. She could taste copper on her tongue, and loud notes were screaming in both her ears. She tried to find the staff with her hands, but they stung and tingled and wouldn't move like she wanted them to.

Her vision was the first thing to recover. She could make out the pilot, crumpled in a pile on the far end of the ship. She wondered idly if they were even still alive and wasn't sure if she cared. Also, she made a mental note to remember that melody but never use it near wet or metallic surfaces.

The ringing had finally begun to fade when she noticed that the pilot was getting up. Not steadily at first, and though they seemed to have gotten the worst part of it, they were struggling to their feet and looking around. Sjora realized with horror that the pilot was looking at her.

She took a deep breath and rolled over to her hands and knees, finally spotting the staff at approximately the middle of the ship. Sjora started to crawl and managed to stand but by then the pilot was already past the staff and still moving her way. The dim lights from the control gave her a first look at the person. He was a man, but with pale tan skin like the people who lived in the Steel Cities on the northern continent. His beard was down to the collar of his shirt, and his expression was ferocious. He was not a man who would willingly submit to capture. He looked like a person who would not think twice about killing a troublesome little girl who got in his way.

Sjora was standing and waiting for him when he lunged for her.

All her years of defensive training came back to her in a flash. He had a knife in his right hand, presenting blade first; she knew how to handle that. As he thrust the knife towards her, she spun to one side, blocking his wrist and punching him in the muscles of his upper arm. He growled in pain, and the knife fell from his unresponsive fingers. She stepped on the hilt and slid it away from them both, dropping to her knees and punching him in the inner thigh to weaken his balance, and once between his legs to weaken his resolve.

Another punch landed in his soft belly and she launched herself back onto her feet, driving her head into his chin to send him sprawling. She heard the crunch of bones and teeth but knew she dare not let up for a moment. He grappled for her, but overextended. She dodged his attempt easily and gave him a swift jab to the rib cage to impede his breathing. Ducking her head and rolling, she grabbed her staff and spun back, ready to face him again.

Behind her, she heard a soft mewling sound that she recognized as the pair of vantrell hatchlings. "Well, now I know why you were in our home," she whispered.

He spat a series of insults her way; she did not know the words, but she recognized blind prejudice when she heard it. She twirled the staff between her hands and sidestepped away from the bundle. Her plan was to keep him at arm's length until he wore himself out and then knock him out and bind him. But his plan thwarted hers. He charged at her in a blind fury, taking a pair of strikes to the head and body but managing to pick her up and head for the railing.

The staff fell from her hands and she flailed blindly in her panic, finally feeling cold metal in the palm of her hand as she attempted to throw her over. She grabbed his tunic with her free hand and succeeded in pulling him off balance. Sjora felt her feet floating through the free air, realizing in her fear she had somehow gripped the railing instead. The pilot was not so lucky; she could hear his screams for several seconds as he fell, and then, silence.

She was able to pull herself back into the ship, mostly due to adrenaline, and curled up with the bundle of otherwise healthy vantrells until her body stopped shaking.

As the sun returned to the sky, she had learned the controls on the ship, and turned it around in what she had hoped was the direction they had come. She lowered the altitude and kept her eyes open for the pilot's body. It took another hour to find him, and she set the ship down shakily on the ground and set the anchor pitons to hold the ship steady so she could disembark.

The body had fallen in a grassy meadow at the edge of a small lake. Mountains stood up boldly around the horizon, and deep green trees dotted the landscape.

"Well, whoever you are, you certainly did choose a beautiful place to die," she breathed.

He had fallen face up, she supposed, though the morbid image of his body bouncing once or twice before coming to rest as it had occurred to her briefly. She poked the body with her staff to make sure he was dead. It was not her first time seeing death; as the daughter of the song mistress, she attended every funeral ceremony of her people. But it was the first time seeing violent death. Reassured that he was not going to attack her again, she searched his body for clues to his identity or, for that matter, anything he was no longer going to need.

She found a pouch of coin from the Steel Cities, a weapon of some sort—it reminded her of a description Johen had once given her, something called a pistol—and a necklace with an odd pendant in which was resting a crystal not unlike the ones they used for tracking their animals. When she touched the crystal, a pale bean of light shone out in the general direction of where they had come from.

"This is how you found us," she said softly. "You found a way to track our Compass."

In a pouch he was still wearing across his shoulder, she found a pouch which contained a dozen more crystals, a pair of goggles and a box of small brass cylinders, tapered at one end. These she assumed worked somehow with the pistol, but there would be time later to examine them. For now, she realized that with the dawn her absence would be noted, and they would certainly come looking for her.

She also realized that she was not quite ready to be found. Her eyes returned to the ship, and she saw for the first time a word emblazoned at the bow: Lamprey.

Sjora looked back to the south and decided it was time for her to leave, just as the creatures with whom they were allied did. It was time for her to find her own path, free from the citadel, free from the inevitability of her inheritance. She removed all the items of any apparent value from the dead man and returned briefly to the ship. Lifting the pair of vantrells into her arms, she returned to the broken body and, using strips of cloth from his cloak, fashioned a leash to connect the two creatures. Finally, she removed the crystal from her own necklace and tied it into a collar for one of the creatures.

A few moments later, she re-boarded the Lamprey, retracted the pitons and slowly sailed away. In her mind's eye, she could see the confused faces of her mother and the guards as they put together the uneven pieces of the story of her disappearance. She sighed. She knew she could not run forever, and someday she would return home and deal with the consequences of her actions.

But as she turned the ship north towards the unknown horizons, she told herself that forever was still a very long time.

To be Continued in *Sea & Shadow: Tales of the Dead Man* (book three)

BOOKS BY REN CUMMINS

Tales of the Dead Man:
Steel & Sky (book 1)
Sun & Stone (book 2)

https://www.renwritings.com/
https://www.doceblant.com/ren-cummins/

Mickey Mathews and Barnacle Jimmy

BY JIM SARGENT

Mickey Mathews had no idea he would be talking about pirates that night in his American History class at Michigan Normal College. Arranging his notes on the podium in front of the large room upstairs in Pierce Hall, he glanced at the wall calendar sponsored by Danny's, his favorite diner. Today was April 30, 1945, and the class was entering its fourth month.

As most students heard one way or another, Mathews, who graduated in Normal College's Class of '33, was renowned as a hero on the Hurons' football and baseball teams. A lefty who batted right-handed, he was six feet tall with sandy hair, hazel eyes, and an athletic appearance. As he waited, he watched the two dozen students enjoying a little camaraderie.

At five after seven, Mickey began calling roll. As he checked off the names, two students slipped in late. Giving them a stern look, the part-time professor observed, "I'd appreciate if all of you could make it on time."

The two, a dark-haired, square-jawed young man in a blue shirt and khakis accompanied by a slender coed with brown hair to the shoulders and blue eyes behind horn-rimmed glasses, took the first two desks in the row closest to the window. Neither spoke. They pulled out notebooks and pencils to be prepared for the lecture. Beyond the row of tall windows, the sun had disappeared behind the campus buildings and Ypsilanti's landmark water tower to the west.

Lounging in the back seat of the first row, Frank Tuttle, Mathews' best friend, seemed out of place. The onetime major had retired in 1941 after thirty years in the Army. He and Mickey met that year in Honolulu, when Frank was looking for a renter for his duplex. Mickey moved in, and the two men with much different personalities clicked as friends.

Frank, who stood six-foot-two and weighed 190 pounds, had blue eyes, a rawboned face, and a cinnamon crewcut flecked with gray. Even sitting down with his long legs sprawled in front of him, the longtime officer looked dangerous. He came to his friend's class to hear in a college classroom what he had never learned in high school or picked up in the military.

Closing his roll book, Mickey looked at the students. "Does anyone have any questions? Remember, you were supposed to read the chapter on the New Deal in 1935." No one spoke, although two or three looked around.

Next to Frank, Tommy Jefferson was squeezed into the back seat of the second row. A bulky ex-boxer who was not quite as tall as Frank but who weighed 200 pounds, Tommy had a round face, kinky black hair turning gray, large brown eyes, and a melodious voice that reminded listeners of a blues singer. His smile came easy, and it revealed a missing incisor.

Tommy, the college president's driver, liked to attend Mickey's classes because he never had the opportunity to finish Pershing High in Detroit during the early years of the Twentieth Century.

When the break came at eight-fifteen, Mickey had covered most of President Franklin Roosevelt's "second"

New Deal programs of 1935, notably the Emergency Relief Appropriation Act, which allowed FDR to create the Works Progress Administration, or WPA, the controversial National Labor Relations Act, and the wide-ranging Social Security Act.

When class resumed, Mickey was finishing up on Social Security. Marilyn, the brunette who arrived late, raised her hand. The teacher, always open to questions, looked at her and nodded.

"Mister Mathews, I think I understand what this law means. My grandfather and grandmother live on a farm in Illinois. My mother says they worked from daylight 'until the cows came home.' Mom said when they got too old to work, they didn't even have $500 in savings."

Mickey leaned on the podium, looking at the students. "The value of receiving old-age pensions, or benefits, as they would be called when payments began in 1940, affects the lives of the majority of Americans. Social Security will keep having an impact for many, many years."

"Yes, but…" Marilyn was frowning. "Like you just said, they didn't get any kind of payment until 1940. That was five years later. What happened to the poor people and the older people before then?"

Two or three others murmured their support, and all eyes turned on the handsome instructor. In the back, Frank was thinking, *Okay, pal. How you gonna answer that one?*

Glancing at his notes, Mickey shook his head. "The WPA was created by FDR in 1935 to provide about three million jobs. But even though we know England had 'Poor Laws" dating to about 1600, Germany under Bismarck launched the first social security program in 1889. England passed its National Insurance Act in 1911, and many European countries were passing similar laws.

"Like the English, people in the United States gradually saw the need for government to help take care of the weak and needy. But also like in England, most people saw the weak and needy as 'undesirables,' and they were discriminated against."

Ben, the other student who arrived late, raised his hand. When Mickey looked in his direction, he said, "We don't have that kind of discrimination in America, do we?"

Mickey shifted gears. "You remember how last week we talked about Senator Huey Long, from Louisiana, and some of his 'radical' proposals, starting in 1934?"

"Yeah," said a young blonde in another front seat. Nancy, the coed with curly hair, blue eyes, and too much make-up, was nodding. "Huey Long talked about 'Share Our Wealth,' and I think the book said he was going to tax the wealthy and give it to the average family."

"In other words," said Hubert, who was sitting next to Nancy, "Huey Long was gonna rip the rich. I think maybe he just wanted to win votes. He didn't care about anybody but himself."

Nancy was doodling in her notebook. Turning to the redheaded guy next to her, she said, "C'mon, Hubie. You got that all wrong. Mister Mathews said Senator Long talked about putting a so-called top limit, or 'cap,' on personal fortunes above $50 million. I mean, who needs fifty million bucks? My dad works for Ford, and he's making about 60 cents an hour."

As the color drained from his freckled face, Hubie stuck out his chin. "So *what*? If your old man's smart enough to make more money, he'll find a better job than working for Ford Motors. Everyone knows ol' Henry Ford is one of the biggest cheapskates in America. Henry Ford's a modern-day *pirate*!"

Mickey interjected. "That's an interesting discussion. Actually, what Huey Long proposed, which he modified more than once, was to cap fortunes at $50 million, like Nancy said, through using progressive federal tax laws. The idea seemed to be sharing the wealth with the public through a program of government benefits and public works."

Hubie, wiping his rimless glasses with a white handkerchief, stared at the professor. "Well, I say Huey Long would have robbed people smart enough to be millionaires, to help people who are only smart enough to be factory workers. I call that piracy—robbing the rich to help the poor!"

In the back, Frank was rolling his eyes, and Tommy had a look of surprise on his dark face, but Mickey remained calm. "Look, Hubert, I don't think you know what pirates were in this country. As a matter of fact, I had a distant uncle who was a pirate. Around 1855 in Michigan, there was a Mormon leader turned pirate captain, James Strang. He called himself 'King.' Strang operated around Drummond Island in the Upper Peninsula. But they say ship owners, sailors, dock workers, and fishermen feared him all along the shores of Lake Michigan and Lake Huron."

Alex, a short, blue-eyed student behind Hubert, said, "You're kidding us, right, to make a point about Huey Long?"

"Nope," Mickey said. "Strang was real. My great-great-great uncle on my mother's side sailed with Strang. He called himself 'Barnacle Jimmy' Blackbones, but I looked up his real name. It was James Blair. One of his cousins, Austin Blair, was elected governor of Michigan in 1861."

Glancing around, Mickey could see most of the students were paying rapt attention. "Back to Barnacle Jimmy. After a couple of years, one night, he escaped from Strang's ship when they docked at St. Ignace. He tried to swim across the Straits of Mackinac. A fisherman named Artie Maxwell saved his life. Maxwell and his son fished Jimmy out of the middle of the straits. They carried him home, and Artie and his wife Eleanor nursed the pirate back to health.

"As soon as he woke up, Barnacle Jimmy realized he was nearly in heaven. When asked his name, he said it was Jimmy Williams. To make a long story short, Jimmy recovered in a week. He went to work helping Maxwell on his fishing boat. Artie needed a third man to go with his youngest son, Lester. One year later, Jimmy, who fell in love with the Howes' daughter Juliette, married her in a small ceremony."

Mickey checked his watch. "I almost forgot. A week before the wedding, one of Strang's men, 'Wacky Jack,' escaped the pirate ship, kind of like Jimmy before him. Wacky Jack made his way to the Howes' house, which was near Mackinaw City on the south side of the straits. He spotted Juliette walking on the beach, and he tried to force her. Fortunately, Jimmy, working on the dock, heard her cries. He came to her rescue, and when Jack tried to run, Jimmy slit his old buddy's throat. At first Juliette was appalled, but they were about to get married. So she helped Jimmy drag Jack's body to a dry well. They pushed him in and threw brush on top of him."

Pausing, Mickey looked around. Even Frank and Tommy were sitting up, hanging on his words. The brawny onetime Golden Glover said, "Tell us, Mister Mickey. What happened next?"

As several students turned from listening to Tommy back toward the teacher, Mickey continued: "Jimmy and Juliette got married the following Saturday. Since Juliette had finished grammar school, the following year, she taught him how to write and read, including the Bible. Three years later, he was ordained as a minister. For about ten years he 'rode the circuit,' as they used to say, preaching the gospel. When Juliette's father died, Jimmy took over Howe fishing business. Later, they had three children, two sons and a daughter, all black-haired like Jimmy.

"He and his wife never talked about him being a pirate. Juliette died in 1898, and a year later, Jimmy passed away. Not long afterward, Julie, their daughter, found a letter in her father's hand hidden in a red box in the attic. Jimmy had penned the two-page letter to Juliette while he was away preaching. He reminisced about their life, including the piracy. Frank, the oldest son, published the letter in a Detroit paper. That's how I found out about my distant uncle."

Alex had been listening intently. "So, this Barnacle Jimmy character was a pirate who reformed himself, got married, found religion, and became a father." He brushed back his mop of brown hair. "You can't tell me some lowlife killer like him can change. I'm agreeing with Hubie. I say the weird Barnacle character was a pirate forever."

"I see," Mickey said. "You're saying that a person who starts out with what I'll call a not very impressive past can't turn himself into a better man, no matter what he achieves. In this case, Jimmy was doomed to be a pirate, although he went on to be a father and a minister."

A couple of hands went up, but Mickey held up one hand. "It's after nine o'clock. I'll tell you what. I grew up in Flint the son of an autobody sheet metal repairman and an ordinary housewife. Does that mean I couldn't get myself educated and turn into, say, a writer?"

Alex grinned wickedly. "You used to be a big deal here at Michigan Normal, so now you're teaching this American History class. I get that. You trying to say you're a *writer* too?!"

Mickey looked back at Frank. "Tell them what happened in Hawaii."

Frank was smirking. "Sure, pal," he replied in his deep voice. "I met you in March 1941, when your publisher sent you to Hawaii to write a novel about a possible Japanese attack on Pearl Harbor. We were investigating certain Japanese agents right up until the bombs started falling on December 7, 1941. In a newspaper column, you predicted the attack, but the editor was afraid to publish it. A year later, you wrote your first mystery novel, *Final Secret*. I know. I was *there*."

Several students were gazing at him, and Mickey grinned. "I moved to Ypsilanti late in the summer of 1943. I was asked to investigate threats of espionage at the Bomber Plant in Willow Run made by a Professor Fischer, a Nazi agent. A year later I turned those experiences into my second mystery, *Long Pursuit*. When it was all over, we got to meet Franklin Roosevelt."

In her front seat Nancy, smoothing back her blonde curls, was smiling. "I've got a girl friend who ate at Heart's Delight, downtown. She and her boyfriend heard your wife, Patty, and the big guy's wife," and she pointed back at Frank, "Norma Jean. They were talking about your latest novel. They said you're going to call it *Warm Springs Mystery*."

As the class waited, Mickey said, "We've run out of time. I'm sure all of you have heard enough for one night. We can talk about the late President Roosevelt, who became a friend, and our adventures at Warm Springs next week, once we finish with pirates in Michigan in the 1800s."

A handful of students grumbled about stopping too soon, but everyone stood up, grabbed their books and notebooks, and began leaving. Several smiled at Mickey, and Nancy grinned at Frank.

Outside Pierce Hall, as Frank and Tommy walked with their friend back toward Frank's home on Emmet Street, the former Army major looked at Mickey. "Hey, pal. You never told us you had an uncle, 'Barnacle Jimmy,' who used to be a pirate."

A blue prewar Buick drove slowly past on Cross Street. Afterward, as the three men crossed the street, Mickey gave his friends a quizzical look. "What *uncle* are you talking about?"

A gleam came into Frank's eyes as they strolled past Danny's Diner. "So, you're pulling our leg, right?!"

Mickey, an innocent look on his smooth features, winked once. "Barnacle Jimmy seemed like a good idea at the time. Make sure to remind me of his name before next week's class!"

Tommy's large eyes opened wider. "Man, you sucked me in, *for sure*!" His deep-throated laugh bubbled forth like the water of a brook rolling over stones.

Frank started laughing, and Mickey joined them. They laughed all the way to Emmet Street. When they reached the Tuttle bungalow, Frank observed, "Patty and Norma Jean are going to enjoy hearing about your 'pirate' uncle. Let's go, matey, and hoist a drink to Barnacle Jimmy!"

BOOKS BY JIM SARGENT

Warm Springs Mystery

https://www.jimsargentbooks.com/

Laguna Rana Mugidora

By Barnacle Bill Bedlam

With in the legends in everyone's mind, there's a place that harbors a memory. Every living soul carries a torch–the childhood phantoms that haunt your dreams and sometimes your reality. A glimpse, a tale, a whisper recurring–forever locked in time.

The years of spinning yarns through the bars and townsfolk, the lies become legends and the legends become folklore.

This is one such story.

Deep down in the Delta, below the glades and marsh, a sacred place is hidden. A place of old, a place of fable and fortune that is said to only exist in rumor and hearsay. A place where the air smells like snakes, the brave and the foolish drunkenly boast of its mysteries, but no man dare tread…the lagoon.

Laguna Rana Mugodora is ghostly tucked away in its own tropical oasis, deep in the jungles of an Island known only as Rattlesnake Island. Laguna Rana Mugidora is a fence, a black market for bootleg, a smuggler's cove, and has been rumored for centuries as a pirate's lair and hideaway for a heinous old man. A folk figure from another place another time. From fame to fable he's rumored to be notorious, his name carved in history as an 18th century criminal, a rogue.

A pirate.

As history serves, his name is Bedlam—Barnacle Bill Bedlam as he is known throughout the deep South in legend and tall tale. The Queen of England herself coined Bill Bedlam with the name "Barnacle" for piracy of the high seas and countless acts against the crown. Over time the stories of thievery and depravity surrounded his name-building its brand. He's a larger than life character—a villainous recluse.

The murmurs and slurs still live on the lips of the sailors, fishermen and shrimpers below the Mason Dixon line, spanning all the way to Cuba. They tell eerie stories of passing this fabled Rattlesnake Island from dusk to dawn, where ghostly sightings of a man in black, with long hair, moves through the thicket. Some say they've heard sounds of bottles clanking, the chopping of wood, even pistol fire, and, oh, yes—the rattlesnakes.

Others tell of sighting the smoke bellowing into the night sky from a wood fire deep in the Isle's jungle, while some say they've even heard shanties sung in the distance.

To the working man, the blue-collar fishermen, the shrimpers, those who are true to the sea, and to those who tread it, there's a code we live by…a pirate's code, if you will.

That particular spit of land is taboo, forbidden of outsiders, and every sea-farin' sod that calls the sea his home knows that! There are some things in this world that should not be found.

The true seaman knows his limitations, his life's worth! You must keep to the code.

Beware! Laguna Rana Mugidora lives on to this day—uncharted and un-sung, as an Island of fable, an Island of mystery and rattlesnakes. It's the place on the map with an X that marks the rumor where an age-old pirate lives.

BOOKS BY BARNACLE BILL BEDLAM

The Tales of Barnacle Bill: Skeleton Krewe

https://www.barnaclebillbedlam.com/

The Lure

BY KIRI CALLAGHAN

They'd lost a great deal of blood in their escape from the forests of Arden. Cuts crossed and interlocked like loosely woven threads along their arms and torso. Every muscle ached. The sun so oppressively garish overhead, that the entire sky seemed aflame, while the ground below was nothing but murky shadow.

Learic's eyes were drooping. The air felt torrid, bitter to the taste. The fae fought against their own exhaustion, but their flight drifted lower.

They needed rest, but there was still too much risk of being caught. If the jailor, by some miracle, had failed to take notice of their escape by now; it was only a matter of minutes until half the Unseelie army swarmed every surrounding area in search of them.

Learic's wings wavered. They'd been torn up by the hellish bramble as they'd fought through for freedom. The rest of the lacerations had managed to clot their ever-moving wings, creating more trouble. Drops of crimson streaked along the iridescent. Their breathing shuddered, and they dropped.

The wind bit against their skin as they twisted in the air. Half-asleep but with a desperate attempt to recover from the dive, they found themselves tangled in their own wings before being swallowed in a wave of cold fire.

They sputtered and flailed; their mouth full of salt as they gasped blindly; with adrenaline attempting to renew their vigor. Every cut and gash along their skin screamed, their tired muscles protesting with every strained attempt to keep their head above the water.

Something blunt smacked against the back of their head and stunned, they sank beneath the surface. Their nostrils burned with one drowsy inhale. They choked, their body convulsing before feeling something roughly grip them by the arm, giving a hefty heave.

Their back scrapped unpleasantly against a solid hard edge before they tumbled head first onto the smooth flatboards of a long boat.

Learic coughed violently, rolling awkwardly to the side, feet still somewhat over their head. Another full body cough and the sea water they'd managed to breathe in, found its way out. They heaved, their throat parched and burning, but their lungs were clear.

"Huh," observed a somewhat dumbfounded voice. "*You're* not a mermaid."

"Indeed, I am not," Learic rasped. They blinked rapidly, everything a colorful blur. At last their eyes focused and rested on the only other occupant of the boat: a short-haired woman dressed in a white tunic, cinched at the waist by a gold and blue embroidered sash. "You seem disappointed."

The woman shrugged a little. "Indeed, I am." She cocked her head slightly to the side. "Though I suppose that does make pulling you out of the pool a bit more heroic." She flashed a grin. "You. Are. Welcome." Each word was punctuated with even more pride.

"Thank you," Learic attempted a smile which twinged into a wince as relief dissipated and their body made a point to remind them of their wounds—particularly the dull ache on the back of their head. Their fingers delicately felt around for where they'd felt the initial impact.

"Ah, you're likely to have a bit of a nasty seagull egg there," the woman sympathized. "You hit your head pretty hard on the oar."

"You hit me with your oar?"

"No, *you* hit the oar… with your head," she corrected. "Bit foolish really, you were bound to lose that fight. This is a Brass Gryphon longboat." The sailor affectionately patted the gunwale. "Made from some of the finest oak in all of Terra Mirum."

Learic tried to glare but this expression proved far too painful to maintain. "For the sake of argument…" They shielded their eyes with a hand. "Isn't it possible *you* hit me with your oar by accident as you were rowing?"

"Not really. We weren't moving." Adder pointed to the seat behind Learic, where the oars were locked in place.

"Oh."

"I was giving my arms a rest, having a drink and I heard this *thunk* against the side of the ship and I see all these bubbles rapidly coming up…"

"So you just… reached down and pulled whatever it was onto your boat."

"Yes."

There was a long silence. "Did you say you had a drink?"

"I did."

"Water?"

"Mm."

"Could I?"

"Of course," the sailor reached down by her feet and held out a large waterskin to offer to her new companion.

Learic took it in both hands, shaking, drinking in the surprisingly cold liquid. Like rain seeping into the desert after years of drought.

"I'm Adder," the woman offered. She looked down slightly and reached up to pull the scarf wrapped protectively around her neck down slightly. "And this is Naga. Don't be offended if she doesn't seem friendly. She's just shy."

Learic paused in their drink to look more closely, seeing what appeared to be some sort of small python lazily coiled beneath the scarf. They blinked. "You brought a snake on the ocean with you?"

"Of course I did," Adder answered matter-of-factly. "She goes everywhere with me. Besides, I can't trust her alone in my bunk. She's bound to get into something she shouldn't." There was a small pause. "You didn't tell me your name."

"I didn't," Learic agreed. If the army didn't find them, surely a call for a reward would, and it was ultimately safer to exchange names with as few as possible.

"Ah…" Adder thought a moment and shrugged before digging into one of her other bags. "No matter. I understand not wanting to share. It's pretty common where I'm from. We're all running from something."

"I'm not…"

"Well, flying, I suppose. Now rowing." Adder tapped the side of her nose. "This may come as a shock to you, but I was not born with the name 'Adder'."

The fae took another drink of water.

Adder frowned. "Well, be shocked."

"I…*am* shocked. This is my shocked face," the fae answered dryly.

Adder scrutinized a moment. "It looks very much like your not shocked face."

"Yes, well… my face doesn't move much."

"Ah." This answer seemed good enough for Adder. She held up bandages. "Shall we patch you up then?"

Learic smiled a little in spite of themselves. "I would be very grateful."

Adder moved carefully towards them, scooting to assist. "I personally would not have recommended swimming with these, but the saltwater must have disinfected them marvelously."

The fae winced slightly. "Well, it wasn't actually an intentional swim…"

"Very odd pattern—are they from claws?"

"Thorns," said Learic.

"Nasty thornbush."

"You have no idea."

"May I call you that?"

"Nasty thornbush?" Learic balked.

"I was thinking 'Thorn', but if you prefer…" Adder shrugged thoughtfully. "Or I suppose if you insist on no name at all, I could always call you 'hey you…' but that may get confusing once we get back to the Brass Gryphon. Captain is rather fond of that nickname for me, and I am not looking to relinquish it." She had the adoring energy of a puppy when thinking back on it. "We've got a special bond, Captain and me."

"I… Thorn is fine," said Learic. "Possibly even appropriate."

"Good," Adder agreed. "Thorn it is then."

Learic allowed Adder to work in silence for a moment before curiosity got the better of them. "What *sort* of ship is the Brass Gryphon? Where no one uses their real names?"

"My home. A ship run by more found family than crew," said Adder.

"A fishing boat?"

Adder paused. "We fish… occasionally."

"A merchant boat then."

"We *do* sell things!"

"What sort of things?" Learic asked cautiously.

Adder's gaze averted. "Whatever we find worth… selling."

Learic paused, feeling a sort of sinking feeling in their stomach. "Adder… where do you find these things you sell?"

Adder shrugged. "Bottom of the ocean, ports… other ships."

"You're pirates!" The fae accused, leaning away.

"I prefer to think of us as extreme traders."

"Pirates kidnap and steal—"

"Oh! Do you have anything worth stealing?"

It was the cheerful openness in which the question was asked that threw Learic off more than the question itself. "…no?"

"Then I don't see what all the fuss is about," Adder dismissed. "Now hold still, I'm almost done with these bandages."

Learic fell silent again, their eyes scanning the empty horizon. "Where… is your ship?"

"Oh, some odd miles west."

"Did they leave you?"

"No!" Adder scoffed. "They'd never leave me. Captain loves me. *We* are on a mission!"

"You and Naga are on a mission?" Learic was skeptical.

"And you." She cocked her head to the side. "…Or would you prefer to resume your drowning?"

Learic gulped. "So what are we doing?"

Adder grinned again as she leaned in close. "We, my new accomplice… are going to catch a siren."

It was not what the fae had been expecting to hear. "A siren."

"Yes."

"As in… magical singing voice, lives deep beneath the waves, has hundreds of legends involving the deaths of countless sailors and destruction of ships. That kind of siren?"

"You can't believe everything you hear, Thorn."

"That kind of siren?"

"More or less."

Learic exhaled what might have been intended as a laugh, but sounded more akin to a startled yelp. "And how do you propose to do that?"

"Well," Adder sat back in her own seat. "I have a whole plan… and the first step," she pointed behind them. "Is to reach there."

Learic followed Adder's gaze to the rock that had been named 'the weeping cliffs' for its vague resemblance to someone crying into their hands. It was the massive waterfall and its unusual shape that gave the ocean its name: The Pool of Tears. Docking near it seemed unsafe, let alone attempting to climb the treacherous rocks. "Are we going to them or up them?"

"First to them. Then up them. And at last, on them." Adder pointed to a dark inlet behind the weeping head that looked like it might be a small cave. "There specifically."

"I see. How are we going to accomplish that?"

"I have rope, and a grappling hook, and love on my side."

"Oh good," Learic laughed nervously. "I was worried it might be some vague method of execution likely to end in death."

"Nope." Adder tapped her temple smartly with her index finger. "Always thinking."

The fae cleared their throat before attempting to sound reasonable and keep the 'if you do this, you will die' tone out of their voice. "Flying would be faster. And *safer*."

"I'm afraid I lack the bone structure or mechanism for that type of travel," Adder commented, further examining her bag as if she expected to find something that would aid in this new suggestion.

Learic blinked, took a deep breath and tried again. "I could fly you up there."

Adder raised her eyebrows. "You could?"

The fae extended their wings. The blood washed by the saltwater, they cast a rainbow-like mosaic of light on the boat and across Adder's face.

"Those aren't just for aesthetic?"

Learic stared, incredulous.

Adder shrugged. "Beauty is not to be neglected." She ran a hand through the short deep royal purple strands of her own hair, seeming to pose with her head cocked back. Despite the somewhat ridiculousness of the moment, Learic had to admit it did show off the bone structure of her jaw and cheekbones quite marvelously. "I myself don't grow this color naturally, you see." She snuck a peek at Learic and paused. "Are you shocked right now or is this your normal face again?"

"Shocked, positively, I assure you," said Learic absolutely deadpan before clearing their throat. "But, my wings are purely for utilitarian use. I'm a bit… exhausted but I'm sure with a little rest while you row us a little closer, I should be able to get us up there just fine."

Adder smiled slightly. "Really?"

"Yeah, well… you saved my life and… I'm pretty sure if I let you climb those rocks alone, you're going to fall horribly to your death."

Adder thought a moment and nodded. "Fair enough. Swap me seats so I can row again?"

"Agreed."

As Adder and Naga settled back into the rowing seat, she nodded to the bag now by Learic's feet. "Help yourself to some rations."

Learic gave an appreciative smile before retrieving a roll from the bag. "So. Rowing away from your crew. Alone.

Set to scale treacherous cliffs and fates know what else. All of this for love?"

Adder's smile softened, her voice holding a weight to it Learic had never heard before. "Don't all the best adventures start that way?"

"I wouldn't know," Learic admitted.

Adder tapped her nose again. "Well, then you best pay attention, my fine colorful friend, this will be quite the learning experience for you…"

"Who is the lucky person?"

"Me," said Adder. "Lucky for being in her light. For hearing the melody of her voice every day. For being able to make her smile." The sailor smiled dreamily and paused in her rowing to muse over the memory of her love. "But to answer what I think was the intent of your question, Lark is the name of the unfortunate recipient of my affection."

Learic's face crumpled. "Unfortunate?"

"I know who I am, Thorn. And I know she deserves the best…"

"So she sent you on this mission to prove yourself?" Learic couldn't help but feel a little disgusted.

"Oh, not at all. She tried to stop me."

"Stop you?"

"They all did. Well, except perhaps Captain. But that's because he knew I had to do this. No one really loves me quite like Captain."

"You know the more you talk about him, the less convincing it sounds…" Learic muttered half under their breath.

"I sent myself on this mission," Adder said firmly. "I'm the one who decided to leave. I'm the one who stole the long boat to get out here."

Learic blinked hard. "But if no one sent you, why in Fate's name would you ever—"

"Because she deserves the best. And since I am not the best, I will do everything I can to give her the best...." Adder trailed off, seeing the confusion on Learic's face. "You've never been in love."

"No."

"It makes a fool of everyone," Adder explained, then, with an impish grin, "But I was already a fool."

Learic laughed. "I don't know if that really gives you an advantage..."

"Agree to disagree," Adder looked over the side of the long boat before locking the oars into place again. "There's some reefs here, we'd be safer to anchor and fly from here if you can manage." She secured a rope around one of the oars and dropped the other end secured to a weight over the side.

Thorn finished their roll and looked up to the ledge Adder had indicated before. "Yeah, I think we can manage that."

Adder donned a small satchel, careful to not place the strap over Naga.

"Are we... bringing the snake?"

"Of course. Where I go, Naga goes. Besides, I can't leave her in the boat, she's not old enough to row."

"Adder..."

"I know, I know... she doesn't have thumbs either."

"No, I just..."

"Are you afraid of the snake?"

Learic hesitated. "No... I'm concerned... of being possibly *bitten* by the snake."

Adder snickered.

"What's so funny?"

"No, I'm sorry, there is no way you could know..."

"Know what?" Learic sighed.

"Naga cowers from an abrupt breeze. She's not going to strike you. You won't even notice her," Adder assured, tucking her scarf carefully around the small ball python.

"Alright…" Learic carefully stood and hooked their arms under Adder's, gripping their own hands to hold her to them. "Ready?"

"Let's do this."

Learic's wings launched them both up into the air with some momentum before the weight of two people caught up with them. Their pace slowed but they did not fall. Their fingers dug a little into Adder and they focused on their breathing.

"Am I too heavy?"

"What? No, I'm just not used to carrying people… and I'm injured."

"Ah, fair point. Shame you had to fight that thorn bush before we met, eh?"

"Can we please stop talking until we get up there? This is a lot harder than it looks."

"Right," said Adder and clamped her mouth shut. She then proceeded to make a sing-song noise with her lips pressed together that sounded suspiciously like, 'my lips are sealed.'

They had to fight against the wind currents, but with a little effort and direction from Adder's enthusiastic head gestures, they landed on the ledge.

Learic expected to see some entrance to an underwater cave or a pool of some sort, but instead they saw a great bird's nest. Golden feathers were scattered about, both shed and built into the nest itself.

Adder patted Learic to be released. She moved with a quiet caution, taking a moment to look around, before climbing into the nest itself. She picked through its construction, searching for something in particular.

Learic's brow furrowed. "I don't understand…" They stared at the large unbroken eggs. Eggs nearly as tall as Adder as she poked around them but otherwise ignored them entirely. "I thought we were after a siren."

"We are," Adder answered from her hands and knees. "And when fishing for such a rare catch…" She sat up to hold up a perfectly formed golden feather. It glittered in even the slightest light, humming with magic. "One needs a proper lure."

Learic smiled, confused but charmed.

Adder pushed herself up, her scarf slipping from her neck as she adjusted the satchel strap, before putting the feather inside.

Learic's smile dropped instantly. "Adder, where's Naga?"

Adder's hand flew to her neck, finding nothing, the panic on her face was clear. "Oh no, baby where are you?"

The hair on the back of Learic's neck prickled a moment before they heard a chilling cry. As if an eagle could roar. They swallowed, seeing a golden shape in the near distance of the sky. "Adder, we have to go."

"Not without Naga," Adder insisted, digging through the nest carefully.

"Adder—" Learic moved towards the far corner of the ledge as the approaching form landed in the shadow with disturbing quiet. Dark eyes locked on them.

Neither pirate nor fae had seen a griffin up close and it was far larger than they'd imagined. Its golden coat, much like the feather Adder had held up was glowing with magic, catching every hint of light that hit it.

"Adder," Learic whispered, both afraid to move and trying to inch further away. "I don't think she's going to be very happy with you so close to her eggs… we need… to… run."

The griffin's head cocked to the side, eyes narrowing, making a strange little irritated growling chirp.

Adder finally found Naga exploring the twigs, having nestled deep inside and sighed in relief. "Found her!" She carefully retrieved the small little snake, gathering her into her arms and stood, finding herself face to face with the griffin. "Oh… um… hello…"

The griffin screeched.

"We uh, we got lost? You have a lovely home here, we were just leaving…Are these your kids? So cute." Adder carefully and as surreptitiously as possible tucked Naga into her satchel, securing the latch without breaking eye contact with the griffin as it stalked towards her. She stumbled out of the nest, and with that brief moment of not keeping eyeline, the griffin flapped its wings angrily, the force throwing Adder off the ledge.

Learic dove after her, folding their wings to try to catch up. Their arms outstretched, fingers grasping before at last finally wrapping their arms around Adder. Their wings extended just in time to catch the wind currents rather than smacking into the rocks, and safely gliding down towards the boat.

"I… thank you!" Adder stammered gratefully, shakily stumbling to her seat.

"Less thanking, more rowing," Learic urged, pointing up to the griffin on the ledge.

"Oh dear." Adder unlocked the oars as Learic pulled up the anchor weight.

The griffin swooped down, the same strange screech echoing against the cliffs as it dove towards the boat.

"Row, row, row—" Learic urged.

"Your boat, gently down the—"

"Adder!"

"What? I thought we were singing…"

A great wind rushed over their heads, catching the wings of the griffin, shoving it back towards the cliffs with a supernatural force.

"How in Fate's name did that happen?" Learic paused. "That… noise. What is that noise?"

Adder stopped to listen, hearing a faint song on the breeze. She smiled and looked into the wind's direction, seeing the shadow of a large steam ship approaching. "Sweet salvation." She looked back to the real griffin who, seemingly unharmed, appeared dazed by the song. She turned the boat around and began rowing back to the ship known across the seas as the Brass Gryphon.

"She's alive!" A voice called from above. "And she brought someone with her!"

Chains lowered from the side of the ship and Adder indicated to Learic how to secure them to the boat so they could be lifted up.

"Um… is it alright that I'm…" Adder waved dismissively at Learic before they could finish their sentence.

"It's fine. As far as I'm concerned, you're officially part of the family," said Adder.

"Family?" the word seemed to dumbfound the fae.

"Of course. You do know what family is, don't you, Thorn?"

Learic's mouth quirked ever so slightly. They looked down a moment. "Only in name, really."

"Adder, you idiot, we thought you were a goner for sure!" One pirate laughed, reaching a hand to help her out of the boat as it rose above the rail. "Captain was taking bets on if we'd even find your bones."

"Liar," Adder laughed. "Captain loves me. Right?" She looked around to find a confirmation, or even the captain himself.

"We didn't expect to find more than one of you," commented another pirate.

"Oh! Everyone, this is my new friend Thorn. They saved me from certain death and Naga from being an uncertain breakfast. And if they'd like to stay... I'd like to nominate them to join the crew. They've already proven to be extremely clever and reliable."

Learic's mouth hung slightly agape. "But you don't even really know me."

"I know what's important," said Adder. "Everything else will come when you want to tell me."

Learic wasn't sure what to say. Their mouth opened and closed several times without words finding their way out. Finally they found their way to a simple, "Thank you."

"Adder..." A woman with teal hair walked into the small crowd. Her voice was melodic, as if every word was sung. Her skin had an iridescent sheen, and Learic could almost see what looked like the faint hint of scales around her ears and down the back of her neck. "I'm glad we made it in time."

Adder's natural smile somehow seemed to widen at the sight of her. "You came to rescue me."

Lark's eyes averted. "I convinced Captain it would be ill-advised to leave you behind."

"She hijacked my ship!" Barked Captain Lorinae as he came down the stairs from the deck above, with what looked like half a shackle dangling from his wrist. "I should try you for attempted mutiny."

"You're fine, and so's the ship," Lark glared back at him.

"You care about me," Adder mused.

"What?" Lark looked at the other woman like a startled cat. "No, I see you as an invaluable asset to the crew. We stick together—"

"Oh, this is so embarrassing for you," Adder teased.

"Shut up," said Lark, floundering for a sense of superiority. "I was just… I felt guilty. I didn't think you'd be stupid enough to actually chase a griffin—"

"Just to bring you one of its feathers?" Adder finished, producing the feather from her satchel. Naga poked her head curiously out of the bag as the flap lifted.

Lark's eyes widened. "You…you actually succeeded?"

"For you there is little I cannot accomplish."

"Adder…"

"See for yourself if you doubt me," Adder offered the feather to Lark. "Legend says griffin feathers hold the power to even cure the blind—you'll see truth itself. I will be unable to lie."

Lark reached out and gently pushed aside the feather so her view of Adder was uninhibited. "I don't need a talisman to see you for what you are."

Adder's gaze lowered.

"Impulsive, reckless, and annoyingly thoughtful, and… I would be absolutely lost if something happened to you."

Adder looked up abruptly. "I'm sorry?

"Don't make me repeat it." Lark looked down, unable to keep the other woman's gaze. "You are a rare treasure."

Adder's grin returned. "May I kiss you?"

"I really wish you would.

Adder wrapped Lark in her arms, hesitated in anticipation and gently kissed her, bending her back into a dip. It was a sweet moment that seemed surrounded by silence despite the great whooping and cheers around them.

As they rose back upward, and the world came back into focus, both women felt the congratulatory back pats and hugs of the crew around them. Lark's eyes finally settled on Learic and she laughed. "We might have broke your new friend, Adder. They look quite shocked."

Adder glanced back and grinned. "Thorn! Your face is fixed!"

BOOKS BY KIRI CALLAGHAN

Alys

https://www.kiricallaghan.com/

About the Authors

(IN ALPHABETICAL O RDER)

Barnacle Bill Bedlam is a one-of-a-kind author whose brand speaks for itself. This scallywag shares his "tall tales" of plunder and pillaging throughout the Golden Era of Pirates. Barnacle Bill's book series, which include *Pirates 'n Poets* and *Skeleton Krewe*, are unique fantasy tales sent in the 18th century Caribbean. For YA readers and up.

David K. Bryant is one of the top historical fiction authors of our time. His books present believable characters in historical plots that reflect occurrences happening throughout time. *Dust of Cannae* looks at the annihilation of the Roman army long before Caesar's days. *Beyond the Last Hill* resolves to discover what sinister event lurks in Cold-War England.

Kiri Callaghan Born from ink and stardust, Kiri Callaghan enthusiastically prods and catalogs the world around her. She's driven by questions: the why's and what if's of life. Her novels take the reader down a rabbit hole filled with the curiosities of fantasy and adventure. After all, Kiri is curious.

Teresa Carol leads the reader on adventures with the supernatural. Her books, *All Spooked Up* and *How to Spook Yourself*

Up are designed to help the paranormal investigative enthusiast that that next step into working with ghosts.

Ren Cummins is a well-known, multi-talented writer whose forte is to create plausible worlds filled with monsters, airships, heroes, and zombies in the science fiction and fantasy genres. Cummins' steampunk, sci-fi series takes off with *Steel & Sky* and *Sun & Stone*, the first two books in the series: *Tales of the Dead Man*. For YA readers and up.

A. M. Crane is well-known for spine-tingling tales of the supernatural. Crane's book, *Sullivan House*, is loosely based on haunting events that occur in historical Savannah, Georgia.

Marti Melville is known for her pirate series, *The Déjà vu Chronicles*, and her *BallyHuHu* children's books. Melville's approach to historical, paranormal fiction is based on historical "possibilities." Her pirate books are filled with twists that take readers on life and death adventure. Melville's children's books are based on a belief in creativity and encourage kids of all ages to "Use your imagination."

P. J. Roscoe writes paranormal fiction with an historical twist. Her award-winning books, *Echoes*, and *Diary of Margery Blake*, captivate readers with spell-binding history and a dramatic look at women's issues.

Jim Sargent is a retired professor, an expert on U.S. History, and a longtime writer. His book, *Warm Springs Mystery* engages the reader in a mysterious crime fiction that is based on history from the 1940s.

T. L. Vale magically brings to life the awareness of psychic phenomenon and spiritual gifts possessed by all people. Her *Emma* series is a fictional illustration of the discovery of a young girl's encounter with magical gifts. For YA readers.

About Doce Blant

Doce Blant Publishing™ believes in creativity. Working together with our authors, we strive to support bright and imaginative minds through publication.

Doce Blant Publishing™ is a small house press created to support the new author, while providing quality stories to passionate readers.

We believe in the following values:

EDUCATION • SUPPORT • OPPORTUNITY • TRUST

https://doceblantstore.com/
https://www.doceblant.com/

Federal Way, WA
Established 2015

www.ingramcontent.com/pod-product-compliance
Lightning Source LLC
LaVergne TN
LVHW011707060526
838200LV00051B/2797